Tyrone's Betrayal

Books in

THE ROOSEVELT HIGH SCHOOL SERIES

Tyrone's Betrayal

THE ROOSEVELT HIGH SCHOOL SERIES

GLORIA L. VELÁSQUEZ

PIÑATA
BOOKS

PIÑATA BOOKS
ARTE PÚBLICO PRESS
HOUSTON, TEXAS

This volume is made possible through grants from the City of Houston through The Cultural Arts Council of Houston/Harris County and by the Exemplar Program, a program of Americans for the Arts in collaboration with the LarsonAllen Public Services Group, funded by the Ford Foundation.

Piñata Books are full of surprises!

Arte Público Press
University of Houston
452 Cullen Performance Hall
Houston, Texas 77204-2004

Cover illustration and design by Vega Design Group

Velásquez, Gloria L.
 Tyrone's Betrayal / by Gloria L. Velásquez.
  p.   cm. — (The Roosevelt High School series)
 Summary: Angry and troubled when his alcoholic father abandons the family, high school senior Tyrone gives up his plans to become an engineer, drops out of school, and takes a full-time job, refusing help from his girlfriend, school counselor, and a psychologist with problems of her own.
 ISBN-10: 1-55885-465-7
 ISBN-13: 978-1-55885-465-9
 [1. Family problems—Fiction. 2. Dropouts—Fiction. 3. African Americans—Fiction. 4. High Schools—Fiction. 5. Schools—Fiction. 6. Alcoholism—Fiction] I. Title. II. Series: Velásquez, Gloria L. Roosevelt High School series.
 PZ7.V488Tyr 2006
 [Fic]—dc22   2006043240

♾ The paper used in this publication meets the requirements of the American National Standard for Information Sciences—Permanence of Paper for Printed Library Materials, ANSI Z39.48-1984.

6 7 8 9 0 1 2 3 4 5   10 9 8 7 6 5 4 3 2 1

For the Male Voices Project
and
my special friends, Rudy Santos Gutiérrez,
Pedro Arroyo, and Jerry Burge, in acknowledgment of all their
hard work and for serving as positive role models to our
underrepresented male youth.

ONE

Tyrone

They're at it again, I think to myself, pulling the blankets over my head, hoping to drown out the angry voices coming from downstairs. But the voices keep on getting louder until there is a crashing sound that worries me even more. Bewildered, I come out from under the covers, carefully opening the door and making my way out into the dark hallway.

"I can't take this anymore. I have to go," Dad says gravely as I watch in silence from the top of the stairway. He is standing at the edge of the living room facing Momma, who is wearing her faded purple housecoat. Momma's favorite porcelain rooster is lying on the floor in pieces next to the overturned table that once held Momma's collection of farm animals.

Reaching out for Dad's arm, Momma cries, "No, Jerry, please don't go. Please wait. I know they'll give you a better job soon."

When Dad lifts up his face, the lamplight shines on his glazed eyes, and I know that he's had too much to drink.

"How long have they been saying they'd hire me full-time? It's going on two years now, Margaret. Well, I've

1

done had it. I'm sick of their promises! I ain't gonna do this no more."

Jerking his arm free from Momma's grasp, Dad turns around, but Momma quickly steps in front of him, begging, "Jerry, please don't go. Do it for the kids . . . please."

With a muffled cry, Dad turns away from her, then the next thing I hear is the front door as Momma slumps to the floor, sobbing. I want to run downstairs to comfort Momma, let her know that I'm here for her, but there's a nervous confusion in my mind that won't let me think clearly. Turning to go back to my room, I catch a glimpse of Zakiya, who stares at me sadly through her cracked bedroom door.

As I climb back into bed, my ten-year-old brother, Jerome, calls out to me from the small bed where he sleeps next to the closet.

"What were you doing?" he asks sleepily.

"Nothing," I answer. "Go back to sleep." I stare into the darkness, wondering if Momma is still on the floor crying or if she's gone to bed.

The next morning, Zakiya's loud, annoying voice awakens me through the opened door. "Momma says it's time to get your black butt out of bed!"

Jerome's empty bed tells me that I've overslept. I quickly grab some clothes, then hurry down the hallway to the bathroom, hoping Rudy is late to pick me up.

Once I've showered and dressed, I splash an extra dose of Old Spice on my face, thinking I better shave by tomorrow or Maya won't like it. Maya and I have been together since she first came to Roosevelt during my sophomore year. It's never bothered her that I'm Black. When we first started dating, I was the one who had problems with her being a Chicana, but now I'm cool about it.

Downstairs, Momma is seated at the kitchen table drinking coffee while Jerome is finishing up a bowl of cereal. Momma's eyes are red, and she looks as if she hasn't slept. "We're out of milk," Momma says in a hollow, lifeless voice.

I want to ask her about last night, about Dad, but I can't. Not in front of Jerome. As I reach for a Coke from the fridge, a horn honks, so I mumble good-bye to Jerome, who is bothering Momma about why he can't have a Coke for breakfast.

Outside, I slide into the backseat of Rudy's car as Tommy, who is sitting in the passenger seat, asks, "Are we picking up Maya this morning?"

"Yeah, *buey*, are we?" Rudy asks, steering the car away from the curb in the direction of Roosevelt High, which is only about a mile from our apartment complex. These days, Rudy likes to call everyone *buey*. Maya says it's supposed to be funny because it literally means an ox.

"Maya and Ankiza left early because they had a senior class meeting," I explain. "That must've been why Juanita wasn't home when I called her," Rudy says as he turns up the radio.

I guess you can say that Tommy, Rudy, and I have been best friends since junior high. We respect each other like brothers. We've always watched each others' back and done things together. Now we're all bad-ass seniors.

As we approach campus, Rudy rolls his window down so he can check out a group of freshman girls. Whistling like a coyote, he yells out, "Hey, baby dolls!" When one of them gives him the finger, Rudy laughs back at her, rolling up his window with a sleazy grin.

Tommy frowns at Rudy. "Better not let Juanita catch you doing that."

"Nothing wrong with lookin', right, Ty?" Rudy asks, staring at me in the rearview mirror.

"Yeah, sure," I agree, knowing too well that Maya wouldn't like it if I talked smack like that with other chicks.

Aware that something is bothering me, Tommy turns around to ask, "What's up with you, Ty? You're too quiet."

Rudy flashes me another sly grin through the rearview mirror. "Leave him alone. He's thinking about those cute baby dolls we just saw." Rudy chuckles, rolling his window back down so he can check out some more girls.

After we've parked the car, we take a shortcut across the football field to the main building. Roosevelt High is an okay school, no gang shootings or stuff like that, but it is kind of snobby, like the rich people who live in Laguna. Sometimes I wished I lived in San Martin or one of the surrounding cities. They seem more like the real world, unlike Laguna where you don't see very many Blacks or Chicanos, mostly white kids, some Asians, and a few Middle Easterners.

At my locker, I grab my books for my classes. Then I join Tommy at the end of the crowded hallway and head to the Math building for first period algebra. When we get there, Mr. Bukowski, or Mr. B. as we all call him, is at the chalkboard writing our daily problems. As I walk through the middle row to my desk, I accidentally trip over Cal Romero's backpack, which is blocking the aisle. Apologizing, Cal reaches down for his backpack, but not before I give it a swift kick under the next seat.

Startled, Cal frowns, "What'd you do that for?"

Then Jonathan, the class jerk who is sitting next to Cal, snickers loudly. I reach over and grab Jonathan by the collar, raising my fist in his face. "What's your problem, jerk?"

One of the girls behind me screams as Cal jumps to his feet to separate me from Jonathan. Tommy rushes to my side, but by now, Mr. B. is there pulling me away from Jonathan, whose face is flushed with fear.

"That's enough," he demands. "Go back to your seats and get started on today's assignment." Then Mr. B. takes me out to the hallway. His bulging blue eyes drill into me. "What in the Sam Hill got into you, Tyrone? You know fighting isn't allowed at our school. You could get expelled for this. Have you forgotten this is your last year at Roosevelt?"

There is a sinking feeling in the pit of my stomach as I realize how much I've disappointed Mr. B. He's always been one of my favorite teachers at Roosevelt, even though I've had problems with math since I was in junior high. But Mr. B. is one of those teachers who really cares about his students. Mr. B. is always around after school, and he never talks down to us.

"I should report this to the dean of students, but I'm going to let you slide just this once. Understand this," Mr. B. threatens as I avoid his eyes, "if it happens again, there'll be consequences. Now, what just happened?"

Shaking my head, I wait for another lecture from Mr. B., but he orders me back into the classroom. Everyone stares as I quietly take my seat. The minute the bell rings, Tommy follows me out of the classroom. "Are you okay, Ty?" he asks as we continue down the hallway.

"Yeah, I'm cool. Don't know why everyone got so excited."

I shrug as we part ways for our next class. When I get to economics and I open my book, all I can think about are Momma's swollen eyes and the crushed look on her face. I don't hear a single word of the teacher's lecture as I think about what happened last night.

At noon, Maya's waiting by my locker. Her face is rigid. "Ty, I heard you almost got into a fight," she begins. "What was that all about?"

"Nothing, baby," I reply innocently as I open my locker, wondering why Maya thinks she can run my life. Maybe it's because we've been together for such a long time. We've only broken up once, when Maya was having problems with her parents' divorce, but that still doesn't give her the right to be so pushy.

"Come on, Ty. What's up?"

"*Nada*," I repeat in my bad Spanish pronunciation, slipping my arm tightly around her waist and pushing her up against my locker so I can give her a kiss.

"Stop it, Ty," Maya demands. "We have to go. Everyone's waiting for us."

"Come on, babe. Let's eat alone for a change," I whisper into her ear, but Maya pushes me away, insisting this is our last year to eat with our friends.

When we get to the bleachers, we find a spot next to big-mouthed Rina, who is teasing Sheena about her peanut-butter-and-jelly sandwich. Sheena's the only white person that hangs with us, but she's cool. When Tommy tells Rina to shut up and eat her bean burrito, she starts in on him. Sheena jumps in to defend Tommy and it gets even louder.

Noticing that Juanita is missing, I ask Rudy, "Where's your girl?"

Smiling, Rudy says, "She's with Ankiza. They went to see their counselor about college applications. Me, I'm gonna get a job."

Then Rina throws her empty bag in my face. "Heard 'bout the fight with Mr. Macho. Did you hurt him?"

I answer with a shrewd grin, "No, but I wanted to."

Sheena frowns. "Watch out. You wouldn't wanna get kicked out senior year."

"So what?" I reply.

Maya pokes me in the ribs with her elbow. "Don't say that, Ty. You know how much your parents want you to graduate, especially your mom."

My momma's voice echoes in my mind, always talking to me about finishing high school and doing the things she couldn't do. I'll never forget the time I asked her where I'd gotten Paul for a middle name. We didn't have any Pauls in the family, and it didn't go with my first name at all. Momma's tired eyes brightened as she explained she'd named me after Paul Laurence Dunbar, the African-American poet who educated himself and became a famous writer, even though his parents were slaves. It's funny about Momma, how she only went to eighth grade, yet she reads all this poetry and stuff. Then Momma recited some lines from his poem, "I know why the caged bird sings," emphasizing how this poem captured the hope and strength of African Americans who had to survive the horrors of slavery and prejudice. I didn't think about what Momma said until the day Mrs. Burrows passed out copies of *I Know Why the Caged Bird Sings* by Maya Angelou, explaining that the title came from Paul Laurence Dunbar's famous poem. I guess Maya's right. Momma would care if I got kicked out for fighting because she wants me to be somebody like Dunbar.

I'm pulled away from my thoughts when Rudy cries, "*Híjole*, will I be glad to graduate. No more school!"

"Hey, I'm glad I'm going to San Francisco State," Tommy says. "I can't wait to get away from my dad."

Sheena nods. "Me, too, I can hardly wait to get a job and move out. Mom's ragging on me all the time."

When Rina starts to make fun of the new U.S. government teacher, we drop the college talk and compare notes on our teachers.

After school, Rudy drives me home, and as soon as we pull up to the curb, I look around for Dad's car. It's not there. Jerome is in the living room doing his homework while he watches "Tomb Raiders."

"Where's Momma?" I ask cautiously.

"She's upstairs. Said she's not feeling good. Can you help me with my homework?" Jerome asks as I head for the stairway.

"Later," I answer back, taking the stairs two at a time straight to Momma's room. Knocking lightly, I push the door open and go inside.

Still dressed in her purple housecoat, Momma is lying in bed, and her eyes look puffier than this morning. "Hi, baby. I got a bad cold."

Moving closer to her, I reply, "Don't lie, Momma. I know what happened last night. I know Dad walked out on you and that he ain't coming back."

Collapsing against her pillows, Momma's eyes widen in fear. "Son, who told you that lie? Your dad's coming back. I know he is. He just needs a few days to think. That's all."

"Stop lying, Momma!" I shout back, my voice quivering with anger as Zakiya comes in the room.

"Who's lying about what? What's wrong, Momma?" Zakiya asks, rushing to her bedside.

Watching the two of them together, I realize how much Zakiya looks like Momma: the same coffee-colored skin with wide-set eyes and round cheekbones.

When Momma bows her head, I holler, "Tell Zakiya the truth, Momma. Tell her that no good Dad of ours ran out on us."

"It's not true. Is it, Momma?" Zakiya gently asks.

Momma sobs and covers her face with her hands.

I storm out of the room.

Two

Almost two weeks go by, and Dad still hasn't returned home or even called once to let Momma know where he's gone. I'm dead sure he's not coming back, even though Momma seems to think differently. All she does is talk good about him as if that night never happened. I don't want to hurt Momma, so I keep quiet about it. Anyway, who cares if he comes back? I'd rather he stayed away and didn't hurt us anymore.

Then one afternoon when I walk in from school, I find Momma in the kitchen searching the want ads. There is a desperate look in her eyes, and the warm smile that always welcomed me home is gone. Now Momma's face is hollow and dark like an empty burial plot. "What's that for?" I ask, grabbing a Coke from the fridge.

"The bills will be coming in soon. Got to find me another job. Cleaning houses ain't enough." Momma's been cleaning houses for rich white ladies ever since I can remember. Once when I was around ten or eleven, Momma took me along to do yardwork so I could make some extra money. When we got to the first house, I couldn't believe that only two or three people lived in those enormous Spanish-style homes.

"Told you he wasn't coming back," I tell Momma as Zakiya walks into the room.

"Shut your face, Ty," she orders, giving me a warning look. Ignoring her, I go into the living room to join Jerome, who is watching the snake guy on the adventure channel.

"Have you done your homework?" I ask. Jerome shakes his head, so I quickly reach for the remote and turn off the TV.

"Why'd you do that for?" Jerome complains.

Just then, Zakiya enters the room. "Tyrone, now you're trying to act all bad," she quips as Momma comes in the room.

"Watch your words," Momma warns Zakiya.

Zakiya says, "You're acting like Dad."

I rise to my feet, shouting, "Don't be stupid!" Then I hurry out the front door before I'm tempted to slug Zakiya in the face.

Outside, there is a cool breeze, and the sky is overcast. Wishing I'd grabbed my sweatshirt, I stroll past neighborhoods of townhomes and brightly stuccoed houses until I reach the downtown area. The streets are lined with expensive restaurants, trendy shoe boutiques, and fancy clothing stores where only the wealthy college kids and the tourists can afford to shop. I can't stand shopping, but when I do have to go with Momma, we usually go to JC Penney's in San Martin or to one of the discount stores nearby. Zakiya's the one who loves to go window shopping with her friends downtown. Not me. That stuff bores me.

Crossing the busy intersection on Main Street, I make my way to the 7-Eleven on the corner, and I get myself a Coke. As I approach the entrance, I spot Max, a white guy who graduated from Roosevelt last year. Max is about to climb into the driver's seat of his car when he sees me.

Waving me over, he asks, "Hey, Tyrone, long time no see. What's up? Hanging by yourself on a Friday night?"

"Yeah, sure," I reply, watching cautiously as Max hands a twelve pack of beer through the open door to his friend who I'd never seen before.

Smiling, Max says, "My friend Chad and I are headed to a party. These college babes invited us. Wanna go?"

I wonder if I should go with Max, but it beats walking around feeling dumped on.

"Get in, man. The party's gonna be cool," Max urges.

Then Chad adds, "Don't be a fag. Get in."

Disgusted, I climb into the backseat, knowing that Chad and I are not going to hit it off after what he just called me. One of my best friends is gay, and I never use that word anymore. It's disrespectful even though idiots like Chad use it all the time.

On the way to the party, Max fills me in on his life after high school graduation and the part-time job he tolerates at a dry cleaner's, because it pays for his tuition at the local junior college. "That's where I met these chicks," he says.

Chad makes a dirty remark about girls, which I know Maya would hate. I can't help but think that this Chad guy is a real perve.

The party is in a private house on the north side of town. A college girl named Dora lives there with three of her best friends. Inside, the stereo is blasting hip-hop, and the living room smells like cigarette smoke. Groups of college students fill every corner of the room. Some are crashed on the couch, while others are leaning against the walls trying to talk over the loud music and drinking beer.

Recognizing one of his friends, Chad grabs a few beers from the twelve pack, then he moves over to their side. Max hands me a beer as a chestnut-haired girl walks up to us, introducing herself as Dora. Unable to take his eyes off her huge chest, Max leads her away to a corner where they can talk alone.

Wondering what my next move should be, I take several long drinks from my beer. Just then, I'm approached by two girls who I vaguely remember from Roosevelt. The short, sexy girl, who is wearing the tightest sweater I've ever seen, edges closer to me, saying, "Hi. I'm Micaela, but everyone calls me Mickey. Don't you go to Roosevelt?"

I can feel the heat radiating from her body as I answer, "Yeah, so what?"

Giggling, Mickey's tall, skinny, blonde friend excuses herself as I nervously take another long drink, hoping this will calm my uneasiness.

"Do you want to go out to the patio?" Mickey asks.

I mumble, "Sure," and down the rest of my beer.

The backyard is filled with couples making out. Mickey grabs my hand, and we walk toward the fence. She abruptly puts her arms around my shoulder, bringing her lips up to mine. Then Mickey expertly thrusts her tongue into my mouth. As we begin to make out, Maya's face suddenly pops into my head, interfering with Mickey's sweet taste.

Plagued by guilt, I pull myself away from Mickey, "I need another beer."

Mickey asks me to wait, but I head back inside thinking to myself that she moves way too fast, and besides, I already have a girlfriend. Several minutes later, while I drink another beer and listen to Chad's stupid guy jokes, I catch a glimpse of Mickey entering the room with another guy.

By the time Max drives me home, I'm trashed from all the beer I drank. When I finally manage to unlock the front door, Momma, who looks half-asleep, is promptly at my side. "Son, where were you?" she asks in a worried voice.

"With a friend," I mumble, clumsily moving toward the stairway before she can ask more questions.

Maya calls me on Saturday morning. "I can't believe you did this to me, Ty! We were supposed to go to the movies with Hunter and Ankiza. You know Hunter doesn't come home that often."

After I've offered several apologies, Maya softens up, saying that I can make it up to her tonight by taking her out for pizza. When she orders me to pick her up at seven, I quickly make up a lie about Dad's car being in the garage. Maya falls for it, offering to pick me up.

Momma's cleaning houses all day, so I hang out with Jerome, playing video games and watching MTV. Zakiya, who has gone to a friend's house, doesn't return until Momma gets home. Then, at dinnertime, Zakiya appears in the kitchen, informing Momma that she's eating at the mall with her friends.

Staring at Zakiya's bright lipstick and her tight, short skirt, I snap, "Go wash your face. You look like a ho."

"Shut up, Tyrone. You're not my father," she says as she leaves the room.

Momma remains silent, her face looking bleaker.

When Maya arrives to pick me up half an hour later, Jerome's face lights up with a smile, but I rush outside before Maya has time to get out of the car.

At Rodolfo's, Maya begins to question me again about last night, so I tell her about running into Max downtown. Only, I change the story a bit. I insist he was giving me advice about college classes and I didn't want to be rude, so I ended up hanging out with him the entire evening. Maya quizzes me some more about Max, but I make up a few more lies until she quits ragging on me.

After we're done eating, we drive to Lakeside Park, where Maya finds a secluded spot near the pier. Determined to make up for lost time, I draw Maya into my arms, and we start to kiss. Thrusting my tongue deep into her mouth, I let my right hand slide around to the front of her top until it rests on her breast.

Maya brusquely pushes my hand away, commanding, "Stop it, Ty! You know I won't let you do that!"

"Come on, baby. Just one time," I plead, attempting to draw her back into my arms.

Maya's face is flushed with anger as she slides into the driver's seat. "Don't be stupid, Ty. You know I won't have sex with you or anybody until I'm ready."

"Then I'll find someone who will," I warn her as we drive out of the dimly lit park.

Maya doesn't say another word until we pull up in front of the apartment. "I don't know what's going on, Ty. You're acting like someone I don't know."

On Monday, I'm standing in front of the gym talking with Mickey and her friend, Brenda, when Maya turns the corner with Ankiza. As soon as Mickey sees Maya, she moves closer, leaning up against me.

Glaring at her, Maya says, "Ty, we waited for you at the bleachers."

Before I can offer any kind of lame explanation, Mickey says, "Can't you see he's busy?" Brenda giggles.

Ankiza glares at her. "Maya and Tyrone are going out," she says.

"Sure could've fooled me by the way he was tonguing me at the party on Friday," Mickey answers coyly.

"Shut your face." I race after Maya, who has taken off across the road toward the main office building. Catching up with her, I grab her by the arm.

Maya jerks her arm free. "You and I are finished, Ty." Then she hurries up the steps with Ankiza at her side.

By now, Tommy is at my side. "You're acting like a real jerk, you know that?"

"So what?" I answer rudely. "Like Rudy says, there's chicks everywhere."

Tommy shakes his head sadly as I turn around and head back toward Mickey and her friend.

Three

This entire week has seemed strange since Maya cut me loose. I've tried calling her, hoping to sweet-talk her into taking me back again, but as soon as she hears my voice, she hangs up. So what am I supposed to do? Beg her? Not me. No way will I beg anybody.

And things at home aren't so hot either. Momma hardly smiles, and she doesn't joke around like she used to when Dad was here. I used to enjoy coming home from school. Not that Momma and I talked a lot, but she made it feel like I belonged here. Now it seems like all Momma does is search the want ads and worry about how she's gonna pay the bills.

Even Zakiya's changed. One afternoon she got in my face just because I asked where she was going, so I punched the wall with my fist. Momma started hollering, and Jerome had this scared look in his eyes like the time he fell off his bike and broke his arm. Yeah, things aren't so hot since Dad left.

On Wednesday, I'm about to leave when Momma calls me into the living room. She's watching *Fantasy Dates* with Jerome and Zakiya. "Son, I have good news. I got this housekeeping job at General Hospital. I start tomorrow."

"Oh, yeah?" I mumble. Wish Momma would hurry up since it's getting late, and I'm supposed to meet Max at City Park.

"Only thing is, it's the evening shift. I gotta be there by 3:00 every day."

Glancing away from the phony-looking guy on the screen, Jerome asks, "Who's gonna watch me after school?" There are rays of fear in Jerome's dark-brown eyes as he waits for an answer.

Patting him reassuringly on the hand, Momma explains, "Tyrone's the man of the house now, and Zakiya will be here too."

Zakiya complains about having to come home right after school, so I make a quick exit, slamming the door behind me as I curse under my breath. Why can't Momma understand that I don't want to be the man of the house? She's gotta be sick in the head to think I'd ever want to be like Dad. He's never been a real dad, if you ask me.

At City Park, I spot Max's car near the bathrooms. Relieved that Chad isn't with him, I climb into the front seat, and we drive out of the park. First, we cruise around Laguna until we're bored, then we head over to Max's apartment, which is on the south side of town near the YMCA.

When we get there, he introduces me to his roommate Charles, who is hanging out in the living room drinking beer and listening to alternative rock. The huge stereo system almost takes up an entire wall. Max goes into the kitchen and returns with several cans of beer in his hand. Kevin, his second roommate, walks out of the bathroom. Max offers him a can of beer, but Kevin refuses, insisting he has a paper to write for his sociology class. Grinning like an idiot, Charles calls him a "dweeb." Kevin ignores the remark and goes back into his room to study.

I'm drinking Bud Light and listening to rock music with Max and Charles when I feel the room start to swirl around me. I tell Max that it's time for me to go home. Max is real buzzed himself, so he knocks on Kevin's door, asking him if he'll drive me back to my apartment.

Sounding annoyed, Kevin agrees, and several minutes later we're climbing into his little red Honda. On the way home, Kevin asks me if I'm still in high school, and when I tell him yes, he says, "It's none of my business, but aren't you kind of young to hang out with Max?"

"You're right," I answer. "It's none of your business."

After that, we're both silent until we reach my apartment. When I thank Kevin for the ride home, he politely replies, "You're welcome."

Thursday morning, I decide to ditch school. Instead of going to Roosevelt, I take the bus to Max's apartment where I hang out until he's finished with his classes. Then, we spend the afternoon watching talk shows and drinking beer.

I do the same thing on Friday, and Momma never even notices. She's always tired now from working nights, so she rarely gets up in the mornings with Jerome anymore. At night, I make sure I'm home before Momma returns from the hospital. Sometimes she'll tiptoe into the room to see if Jerome's asleep, unaware that I've just crawled into bed. Every day I have to listen to Zakiya's threats that she's gonna tell on me, but she doesn't. Maybe Zakiya doesn't want to worry Momma. Who knows? Besides, now that

Maya's gone and dumped me, I deserve to have a good time.

On Saturday afternoon, I'm in my room putting up my new Motown Loverboys poster when Rudy and Tommy drop by to ask why I haven't been in school. "Hey, *ése*, where've you been?" Rudy asks, grabbing my Coke off the dresser and taking a long drink.

"Nowhere," I answer as Rudy burps loudly, offering Tommy a drink.

Shaking his head, Tommy looks at me, his green eyes blazing. "Maya's been asking about you."

Pretending I haven't heard him, I start to brag about the chick I met the other night at Max's, saying, "She's a college babe. Real fine."

"Man, wish I could score like that," Rudy groans, "but Juanita would beat me up if I did."

Tommy's still looking at me sternly. I know he thinks I'm cheating on Maya, but, hey, she's the one who wanted out. Not me.

Singing loudly, Tommy asks if I want to go to the Rock with him and Rudy this evening, but I curtly reply, "Sorry, man, Max and I are going to a party."

"What's this, *ése*? Think you're too good for us now, hanging out with those college *vatos*?" Rudy asks.

Grinning, I tell Rudy he's acting crazy, but the hurt expression on Tommy's face proves he's not convinced by my answer. They hang around a few more minutes, but I don't let them get me down.

When I get ready to go out that evening, Jerome begs me to stay home and watch a movie with him, but I insist I can't, that Zakiya will watch it with him. Jerome gets the saddest look in his eyes as if he's about to cry, so I hastily promise we'll do it tomorrow night. Jerome nods, but I can tell he's still disappointed.

Max and I head out to another party at Dora's where I get trashed again, but this time I don't make it home before Momma returns from the hospital.

As soon as I open the door, Momma gets in my face. "Sure acting like a real man, now, aren't you, son?"

My speech slurred, I lash out, "And how would you know what a real man is?" A look of shock and embarrassment appears on Momma's face. "Don't you talk back to me," she says.

I head for the stairs, leaving her behind in the dark shadows of my anger.

On Sunday, it's almost noon by the time I go downstairs to eat. I'm scrambling some eggs when Momma enters the kitchen. As she begins to lecture me on the evils of drinking, I interrupt, "Leave me alone, Momma. Can't you see I'm no loser like Dad?"

Now Momma's eyes fill with tears.

"Don't cry, Momma," I whisper, pangs of guilt filtering through my veins. "I didn't mean to say that."

But Momma only nods, leaving me alone with my burnt eggs. After that, my day is ruined. I can't even focus on the Lakers game because Momma's hurt face keeps appearing in my mind.

The next morning, I write a note forging Momma's name so I can get admitted back into school. Only now, my classes seem even more boring and pointless. Not even history interests me. Who cares about the Great Depression and all the hungry people? Who cares about my assignments? It's all one big waste of time to me.

By the middle of the week, the word gets to my counselor that I haven't turned in any of my assignments. Mr. Grinde calls me into his office to ask what the problem is.

"It's boring sh—," I stop myself before I cuss in his presence.

Mr. Grinde frowns, emphasizing that I need to pass all of my courses in order to have enough credits to graduate. When I shrug my shoulders, Mr. Grinde sighs in frustration.

As I get up to leave, Mr. Grinde says, "Remember, Tyrone, I'm here if you need someone to talk to."

Avoiding his concerned stare, I thank him, going back out into the hallway. I've only taken a few steps when I run into Maya and Rina. They're coming out of the bathroom, and they're headed toward the counseling offices. Pausing in front of me, Maya says, "Hey, Ty, you missed the senior class meeting."

"Yeah, so?" I answer, trying to sound like some bad-ass guy.

Rina punches me lightly on the shoulder, saying, "Stop acting like a jerk! You're not gonna graduate with that attitude."

Maya still hasn't taken her soft brown eyes off me. "Ty, please talk to me. Why do you insist on behaving like that?"

When Maya reaches out to place her hand on my shoulder, I move away from her, leaving her with a stunned expression on her sweet face. As I race out of the main building, I kick myself, wondering why I tripped that way with Maya. She was so sweet with me, and she looked so fine. All I really wanted to do was hold her and tell her about Dad and how miserable I've been without her. Instead, I tripped out.

When I get home, Zakiya is in the living room watching Oprah. Just as I'm about to ask for Jerome, the phone rings. It's Mr. Lint, the store manager at Gerald's Drugstore. He explains that Jerome and another boy were caught stealing candy in his store. Then he insists that a parent needs to come immediately to the store to pick up Jerome. Feeling drops of perspiration on my forehead, I hang up the phone and rush out the door before Zakiya can ask any questions.

It is a quick, ten-minute walk to Gerald's. Once inside, I ask the nearest cashier for the store manager, and she points toward a small office in the back of the drugstore. After the first knock, Mr. Lint opens the door and invites me inside. Introducing myself as Jerome's older brother, I glance at Jerome, who is sitting on a chair looking pale and scared. Mr. Lint asks, "Why didn't a parent come for Jerome?"

"Momma works nights, and Dad is away on a trip," I explain to him.

Mr. Lint nods, his bald head glistening, "I see. Well, I'm not going to call the police since Jerome and his friend admitted the truth. I think they've both learned their lesson."

Jerome nods uneasily as I thank Mr. Lint for his kindness, and we quietly exit his office.

The minute we're outside, I explode, "What'd you do that for, Jerome? You know Momma taught us never to steal, not to take nothing from nobody."

Embarrassed, Jerome whispers, "Landon dared me. Please don't tell Momma, Tyrone."

Staring at my little brother, I notice the tears forming in his eyes, and I take pity on him. "Okay," I answer gruffly, "but it better not ever happen again."

When we get home, Zakiya asks, "What was that all about? Jerome, how come you're so late?"

"None of your business," I say. "Did you make anything to eat?"

Zakiya's eyes widen in disgust. "Who do you think I am? Your own private slave? Didn't you know the Civil War done ended a long time ago?"

"Shut up," I answer. Jerome volunteers to make us both grilled cheese sandwiches.

That night, I don't go out with Max. He calls several times, but I keep refusing until he finally gets the point and quits calling.

Four

In the days that follow, I come straight home every day so I can keep a closer watch on Jerome and make sure he doesn't do anything stupid again. Sometimes I help him with his homework, or we just sit and talk about stuff, like the new guys on the Lakers or his basketball card collection. I know Jerome misses Dad badly. I want him to know he can lean on me, to answer his questions and give him advice on not stressing over the hair that's growing on his legs.

"It's a man thing," I explain. "Girls like hairy guys."

Zakiya seems a lot nicer now that I'm home more often, but she still manages to get on my nerves. All she does is talk on the phone with Cassie or Minerva, as if they didn't see each other enough at school. But then again, maybe that's how Zakiya gets it all out. I don't need anybody to talk to, not even Maya. Just me, that's all.

One evening, Max shows up unexpectedly at the apartment, and I'm forced into going out with him and Tom. First, we make a beer run to the liquor store on Peach Street. Then we drive to Tom's apartment, which is near the university. Tom shares a two-bedroom apartment with Vinit, who is a foreign-exchange student from Iran.

Vinit turns out to be real cool. I spend most of the evening listening to Vinit talk about Iranian culture and the Persian language. At least, he's not an idiot like Tom who only likes getting trashed.

It's almost midnight by the time Max drops me off at the apartment. I'm unlocking the front door when I hear a loud, shrill voice call out my name. I turn around quickly as Momma rushes up the sidewalk. Her face is flushed, and she is breathing unevenly as if she's just witnessed a UFO.

"Momma, what's wrong?" I ask as she rushes inside the doorway.

Fumbling with the light switch, Momma cries, "Some man tried to steal my purse." Her body is shivering, and she leans against the wall to steady herself.

"He didn't hurt you, did he, Momma?" I ask, moving closer to her, not caring about the smell of beer on my breath.

Momma shakes her head. Her voice quivers, "It's a good thing the bus driver saw what happened. He started honking the horn. Then he pulled over, but the man took off running before the bus driver could grab him."

"Momma, I told you it was dangerous to take the bus that late at night."

"I know, son," she replies, wiping the sweat from her brow. "Why are you getting home so late on a school night?"

"I'm fine, Momma. It's you who don't look so hot." Then, wishing I could hurt the man who scared her, I ask, "Do you need to see a doctor or something?"

"I'm just shaken up. That's all. Don't need to see no doctor. You been drinking again?"

"I only had a few beers," I say.

"Drinking don't solve nothing," Momma snaps and orders me to bed as if I'm a little kid like Jerome.

The next day at school, I'm walking through the Science building when I meet up with Jonathan. He's with a couple of his idiot friends, but instead of walking past him, I bump his left shoulder. When Jonathan grunts loudly, I don't waste a second. I step toward him and smash my fist into his face, watching him topple to the floor. Before he can get up, I give him a swift kick in the stomach. A crowd gathers around us, and Mr. Beecher, the biology teacher, rushes up to pull me away from Jonathan, whose mouth is bleeding. "Take him to the nurse's office," he orders the two screaming girls next to Jonathan. Then, Mr. Beecher grabs me by the arm, "Young man, you're in serious trouble."

I quietly follow Mr. Beecher to the dean's office. He's not there, so we go to the principal's office. Mr. Marshall asks me to take a seat while Mr. Beecher describes the fight. I know I'm in deep trouble, but I couldn't care less.

Once Mr. Beecher has left, Mr. Marshall says, "Tyrone, you know we have a school policy that does not permit fighting on our campus. I'm going to have to suspend you for a few days."

Then he calls Mr. Grinde into his office to inform him about the suspension. Mr. Grinde shakes his head in disappointment, and I lower my head in shame. Mr. Grinde's always encouraged me to stay in school and go to college. As I follow Mr. Grinde out to the main office, he asks, "Is there someone at home who can come by for you?"

I tell him no, explaining, "Dad's working. Momma's home, but she doesn't have a car."

Falling for my story, Mr. Grinde offers to drive me. When I don't say much on the way, Mr. Grinde tries to calm me down. "You know, Tyrone, it's only a three-day suspension. And I'll make sure you get all your assignments, so you won't get behind. Why don't you tell me exactly what happened?"

"Nothing happened," I answer sullenly, staring out the window at the magnificent Laguna landscape, wishing I were invincible like ancient volcanic mountains, which Maya once told me were sacred to indigenous peoples.

Pulling up to the apartment, Mr. Grinde asks if he can come inside to speak with Momma. When I tell him she's still asleep because she works nights, he backs off, saying he'll call her later. As I open the car door, Mr. Grinde reminds me to call him if I change my mind about talking. For a brief moment, I'm tempted to tell Mr. Grinde about Dad, but I resist the urge, thinking he probably wouldn't understand.

The instant I open the door, Momma calls me into the kitchen, where I find her seated at the table drinking coffee. There are dark circles under her eyes, and her tight curls are pulled back in a short ponytail. "Son, the principal called. What's this about you fightin'? You never done this before. Does this have to do with your daddy leaving us?"

"It has nothing to do with Dad," I defend myself. "Some white guy got in my face. That's all. And I don't wanna talk about it."

Momma's voice is hollow as she orders, "Go to your room, and you make sure you stay there, young man, and think about what you did."

Feeling miserable, I stay in my room listening for Momma to leave for work. After I make myself a tuna sandwich, I go into the living room to watch game shows.

When Jerome walks in the door with Zakiya, she stares at me accusingly and says, "Heard you got suspended for fighting."

"Shut up," I reply, turning toward Jerome, whose eyes meet mine. "And don't you go and think fighting's cool. All right?"

As Jerome nods meekly, I recognize Dad's flat nose and square face. Jerome even has dad's big ears. Too bad, I think. Too bad he has to look like Dad. I'm glad I look like Momma's side of the family.

When the doorbell suddenly rings, Zakiya comes back in the room with Maya, who gives Jerome a hug and asks him about school. Then Maya turns to me and says, "Hey, Ty, can we go somewhere and talk?"

"What's there to talk about?" I shrug, taking in Maya's short skirt that shows off her long, dark legs.

"Come on, Ty. Let's go for a soda or something?"

For once, Zakiya tries to act helpful. "Go ahead, Ty. I'll stay with Jerome."

Glancing around the apartment, Maya asks about Momma, and Jerome tells her, "Momma's at work. She doesn't come home until after I'm in bed."

Grabbing Maya's hand, I lead her toward the door before she can ask any more questions.

At Lakeside Park, I try to steal a kiss from Maya, but she resists. "Ty, I didn't come here to make out. Come on. Let's go sit by the water so we can talk."

Holding hands, we walk to the edge of the water and find a spot where we sit quietly for a few moments, watching the ducks float peacefully in the middle of the lake.

"Why'd you have to hit Jonathan?" Maya asks.

"Because he's a dumb ass," I reply, flinging a rock into the water and scaring away a solitary duck who has drifted away from his flock.

"Come on, Ty. What's really going on? I know Jonathan. He's dorky, but he's not that bad."

Staring into Maya's eyes, I think about how hurt I've been since Dad left, how awful it is to see Momma's despair and the terrible emptiness in the apartment every time I walk inside. Struggling with my emotions, three words come spilling out of my mouth. "Dad left us."

Reaching out for my hand, Maya gently asks me to tell her what happened. Looking away for a few seconds, I blink back my tears, knowing I mustn't cry. Guys don't cry, I repeat in my head. Then, taking a deep breath, I start to describe the night Dad left. When I'm finished, Maya tries to console me by saying, "Ty, I know exactly how you feel. When my dad left, I wanted to die."

"Not me," I stubbornly insist. "I'm glad he's gone. But I need to get me a full-time job so I can help Momma." Then I tell Maya about Momma's big scare the other night and how she was almost mugged. Maya gasps several times as I conclude, "Maybe if I get a job, she won't have to work nights."

"Oh, Ty, you can't do that. You're all set to go to Laguna University. You've always wanted to be an engineer."

"Things are different. I gotta help the family." Then I tell Maya about Jerome and how he got caught stealing, adding, "So I gotta keep him straight too."

Maya continues to plead with me to return to Roosevelt, but I insist I know what I'm doing. After a few minutes, Maya finally gives up, but I can tell she's bothered by my decision. Drawing her close, I give her a long kiss. This time she doesn't resist. When we finally separate, I gaze into her beautiful brown eyes, whispering, "So you're my girl again?"

Her dark eyebrows dart up. "Maybe. But I'm warning you. Stay away from that Mickey girl!"

When I explain to Maya that she's the only girl I will ever want, she gives me a second warning.

"Okay, Ty, but remember, if you get out of line, I'll set Rina Schwarzenegger on both of you!"

Pretending to shudder in fear, I tell Maya, "Come on babe, don't scare me like that!" Watching Maya's serious expression change into a grin, I realize just how lucky I am that she's giving me a second chance.

Five

At first, Momma is angry when I tell her about my decision not to return to Roosevelt. Then all she does is cry, reminding me that I'll be the first in our family to graduate from high school and go on to college. Between sobs, Momma demands I go back to school, but, even though I hate to see her cry, I refuse to change my mind, insisting I'm getting a job. After a while, Momma quits nagging me.

Later, when I walk her home from the bus stop, telling her about all the applications I've been filling out, Momma sadly whispers, "I wanted better for you."

Jerome is also disappointed because I haven't returned to Roosevelt. One afternoon, he asks, "Tyrone, how come you're always harping on me about my homework? If school's that important, why'd you quit going?"

"That's different," I reply defensively. "I gotta help Momma now and be the man of the house."

Zakiya, who manages to eavesdrop even while she's busy gossiping on the phone, cries out, "If you ask me, that ain't being a man. It's being stupid!"

I holler back at her to mind her own business and I go back to helping Jerome with his science project. Who cares what Zakiya thinks? It's my life and nobody's gonna tell me how to run it, not her, not Momma. Nobody.

When Max hears I'm looking for a job, he tells me that one of his friends heard they're hiring at the new Inboxes that opened up near the train station, so that same afternoon, I go fill out an application. I can't believe it when the manager, Mr. Morton, who looks younger than Momma with his pale, unwrinkled face, calls me into his office for a short interview. Although he seems bothered that I'm not finishing high school, Mr. Morton offers me a full-time job, adding that I'll have to work on Saturdays. Thanking him, I fill out some paperwork and agree to begin next Monday.

My first week at Inboxes is chaotic. I'm not sure where everything goes, so I search up and down the aisles until I find the right place for the new supplies. Sometimes, I have to wait on a customer, directing them to stuff they're looking for, and other times I help them get something off the top shelves when they can't reach it. After my daily lunch break, the day whizzes by, and I'm usually home by five-thirty since Inboxes is only a few short blocks from the apartment. The first thing I do when I walk in the door is question Jerome about his homework. Then I crash on the couch until Zakiya says it's time to eat. Still, it seems like I never get enough sleep. I don't get to bed at night until after midnight since I wait for Momma at the bus stop. I don't want anything bad to happen to her again. The hardest part is hearing the alarm go off every morning at six thirty.

At the end of my first week of work, Tommy and Rudy drop by Inboxes where they find me stacking boxes of pencils and pens on the shelves. Pausing to say hello, I say, "I can't talk much because I don't want to get in trouble with the manager."

Rudy gives me his customary Chicano handshake while Tommy says, "Don't worry. We won't keep you." Then he calmly asks, "Ty, why'd you quit going to school? I thought you wanted to be an engineer."

Rudy flicks his chin up slightly, adding, "Yeah, *ése*, what happened?"

Shrugging my shoulders, I answer, "I need the money, and besides, I like my job."

When Tommy looks as if he's about to ask me another question, I abruptly say, "They need me at the cash register." Then I hurry up front to wait on the tall bearded man, who keeps glancing at his watch as if he's late for an important date. I'm ringing up all of his computer supplies when I catch a glimpse of Tommy and Rudy walking toward the front entrance. Rudy flicks his chin up at me as if to say good-bye, but Tommy never even glances my way.

That night, Max calls to invite me out again, but after a few minutes of pleading, he finally gives up, saying, "Dude, you're acting like an old man."

Hanging up the phone, I think about what Max said. Maybe he's right. All I do is work now, six days a week with Sundays off, but that's the day I spend with Maya. Anyway, who cares what Max thinks? Maybe he'll finally stop calling me. I'm sick of Max and his college friends with their party routine. I've got more important things on my mind, like making money and watching out for Jerome.

A few days later, I walk into the apartment to find Mr. Grinde sitting on the couch talking with Jerome.

"Hello, Tyrone," he says, observing me closely as I take a seat on Dad's favorite chair. "Hear you've got a job?"

"Yeah, at the new Inboxes. It's a cool job."

Mr. Grinde's blue-gray eyes pierce into me sharply as he clears his throat to say, "Tyrone, you know I've got you all set up for financial aid at Laguna University."

"Thanks, Mr. Grinde, but I gotta work now."

Jerome glances up from his Super Heroes comic book to ask, "Why do you have to work so much? Why can't you go to school like me?"

"'Cause I gotta help Momma, that's why. Don't you have some homework?"

When Jerome shakes his head and smiles mischievously, I order him to go bother Zakiya for a while. He obediently rises to his feet, promising to return soon.

"I have one just like that," Mr. Grinde comments. Then his voice grows solemn. "Tyrone, it's still not too late to come back to Roosevelt. With some help, you can catch up easily."

Shaking my head fervently, I say, "Maybe later I'll go to college, but right now I can't. Momma needs my help."

Mr. Grinde tries to convince me I'm wrong, but after a few minutes, he sighs and rises to his feet, saying, "Think about what I said, Tyrone, and if you do change your mind, know that I'm here to help you. You're a smart young man, and I'd hate to see all that potential wasted."

After Mr. Grinde leaves, Zakiya comes back into the living room, asking, "What was that all about?"

"He wants Tyrone to go back to school," Jerome answers boldly.

Zakiya flashes a rude look at me and tells Jerome, "Even Celia went back to school, and she was pregnant!"

After I order Zakiya into the kitchen to make dinner, I can't help but wonder if Momma was wrong to name me after Paul Laurence Dunbar.

The following weekend, I march triumphantly into the kitchen waving my first paycheck at Momma.

Glancing at me from the tomatoes she's slicing, Zakiya asks, "What's that?"

I hand Momma my check, saying, "I got paid today. This is for you, Momma."

Drying her hands on the flowered orange blouse she's wearing, Momma takes the check, thanking me. Then in a solemn tone, she says, "Son, I'd prefer it if you went back to school."

When Zakiya snickers, I raise my voice in anger. "Momma, why aren't you ever satisfied?" Then I exit the kitchen, wondering why Momma can't understand I'm doing this for her and for the family.

It's not until we're having dinner that Momma brings up the check I gave her. Sounding apologetic, she thanks me, adding, "It's sure gonna help."

Jerome asks, "Tyrone, do you think you can get me some new basketball shoes?"

Smiling, I happily agree to his request. Then Zakiya interrupts to say she is in dire need of a new winter coat. My eyes meet Momma's, and we both smile as Jerome begins to describe the new Kobes he saw on TV the other night.

That Sunday, when Maya picks me up to drive to the Rialto, I tell her about Mr. Grinde's visit. Her face brightens like a field of California wildflowers. "See, Ty. I told you it's not too late."

"Hold off, Maya. You know I gotta work."

Maya does her best to get me to change my mind, but I refuse to discuss the issue any further.

Hoping to lighten the tension between us, I ask her, "So what's this new chick flick about? You know what I think of sappy love stories."

"Don't be a sludge," she teases, turning onto Main Street and into the new parking lot across from the theater.

We're standing at the snack bar at the Rialto waiting for our popcorn and sodas when two of Maya's friends from the tennis team get in line behind us. Tammy, a short perky brunette, starts talking about college and how exhausted she is from filling out college applications. Then Alexa, who is even taller and skinnier than Maya, reveals that she's going to Brown since that's where her dad went as well as her older brother.

"It's a tradition in our family," she proudly brags.

Tammy asks, "Maya, where are you going to college?"

Maya looks at me before reluctantly commenting, "I'm going to Stanford."

Looking at me, Tammy asks, "How about you, Tyrone?"

Just then our order's ready, and I turn around to pay, leaving Tammy's question unanswered.

With a quick good-bye to her friends, Maya leads me into the theater where we find two seats far off to the side in an isolated row.

As the lights dim and the previews come on, Maya whipers, "Ty, I'm sorry about that."

"Don't sweat it, babe," I reply, trying my best to sound lighthearted, but the truth is the run-in with Maya's two friends has made me feel even more like a failure. As the movie begins, I think about Dad's betrayal and how he totally screwed up my life and Momma's life, too. I hope I never have to see his messed-up face again.

By the time Maya drops me off back at the apartment, I've managed to put Dad out of my mind for a while, but as I walk into the living room, the phone rings. I reach for it, only to hear a familiar voice on the other end of the line.

"Hello, son, how are you?" Dad says cautiously.

There is a sudden tightness in my chest, as if I am being run over by a bulldozer. "I'm not your son!" I cry angrily, slamming the receiver down as Zakiya races to my side.

"What'd you do that for?" she asks accusingly. The phone starts to ring again.

"Don't answer it!" I yell, but Zakiya lunges for the receiver before I can stop her.

"Oh, hi, Dad," Zakiya answers in a honied voice that makes me want to shake her.

"Hang up. Now!" I demand, but Zakiya only glares at me, waving me away as she continues her conversation with Dad.

Now Jerome appears next to her, eagerly asking, "Is that Dad? I wanna talk to Dad, too." Jerome's cheerfulness repulses me as I watch him impatiently await his turn to talk with Dad.

When Zakiya passes him the receiver, Momma walks into the room, and Zakiya happily tells her, "Momma, it's Dad."

Momma pauses, her weary face suddenly alive with hope. Unable to stand it any longer, I give Momma's large plaster rooster a swift kick, and it falls over, breaking in two. Momma gasps and calls out my name, but I'm already halfway up the stairway.

Six

Dr. Sandra Martínez

After several minutes of wandering through the aisles at Inboxes, hopelessly searching for the folders I needed, I decided it was time for assistance. Spotting the handsome African American with the familiar employee's red shirt, I walked up to him and asked, "Can you help me? I'm trying to find the flourescent-colored file folders."

Pausing to look at me, he politely replied, "Yes, ma'am, they're on the next aisle. I'll show you."

As I obediently followed the young man toward the back of the store, I realized there was something vaguely familiar in his ebony face.

"Are you looking for any particular kind?" he asked, coming to a halt next to a wall covered with rows of different-colored folders.

Still searching my memory, it suddenly came to me. "You're Tyrone, Maya's boyfriend, right? I'm Sandra Martínez. We met at my house."

Tyrone's eyes flickered momentarily, but his face remained rigid as he nodded in agreement. Aware that this was supposed to be Tyrone and Maya's senior year at Roosevelt, I asked, "Are you working here after school?"

"Nah, I work here full-time," he answered, pulling a handful of flourescent folders from the racks, which he handed to me.

"These are perfect," I smiled, but before he had time to disappear down the aisle, I asked, "How's Maya?"

Tyrone's face softened into a half-smile. "She's good."

Unable to contain my curiosity a moment longer, I impulsively asked, "Tyrone, aren't you and Maya graduating this year?"

At that, Tyrone's body seemed to stiffen, the harshness returning to his face. "Dr. Martínez, do you need anything else 'cause I gotta finish stacking those supplies?"

It was perfectly clear that Tyrone didn't want to talk about school, so I shook my head, thanking him as he hurried away toward another section of the store.

At the cash register, I furtively glanced around for Tyrone while I paid for my purchases, but he was nowhere in sight.

Determined to get an answer to my question, I went into my office and dialed the Gonzales residence as soon as I returned home.

Maya's energetic voice greeted me, "Hi, Dr. Martínez. Sorry, Mom's not home. She went to a MEChA meeting."

"Actually, I was calling you."

"Cool," Maya replied cheerfully, adding, "Juanita said you and Frank are gonna baptize Celia's baby when it's born."

"Yes. We're absolutely thrilled."

"That's cool. Juanita said her parents are planning a big *pachanga*."

I chuckled at Maya's mention of the word *pachanga*. She sounded so much like her mother. "Yes, Frank's already practicing his *norteñas* with my newest Tigres del Norte CD," Maya giggled. "How are your college plans progressing?" I asked.

"*Bien* cool, I'm still planning on going to Stanford, but I'm sludged 'cause Ankiza changed her mind. She's applying to UCLA. And Juanita's going to Mom's boring university."

Smiling to myself at Maya's assessment of the local university where her mother teaches, I listened patiently, waiting for the appropriate moment to solicit the information I needed.

"Rina's plans are still not sure," Maya added, "but Tommy applied at San Francisco State. He wants to be a boring high school teacher."

"Now, Maya, not all teachers are boring. I'm sure Tommy will make a delightful teacher. But what about Tyrone? I saw him at Inboxes today. He said he's working full-time. Isn't he supposed to graduate this year?"

Maya groaned and began to relate the entire story about Tyrone, how his father had suddenly abandoned the family. "Tyrone's been weird since then. He insists he has to work full-time to help support the family. His mom even had to get another full-time job. She works nights at the hospital."

"I'm very sorry to hear about Tyrone's troubles," I remarked, imagining the tremendous burden Tyrone was carrying inside his heart.

"Yeah, I've tried talking to him, even Mr. Grinde the counselor tried, but he won't listen to us. And Ty was all set to go to Laguna University. Do you think maybe you could talk to him?"

"Yes, of course I will, but I'm not sure if he'll listen. It sounds like Tyrone's already made up his mind. Why don't you give me his home address? If I remember correctly, he lives near Juanita."

"Yeah, he does," Maya eagerly replied, saying Tyrone's apartment number into the receiver. "Dr. Martínez, you're the coolest. Wish my mom were more like you," Maya said before we hung up, which made me smile.

While Frank and I were having dinner that evening, his face grew serious when I told him about my plans to speak with Tyrone. "Hon, are you sure you have the energy for this? I mean, we just lost the baby and then all that time you spent helping Celia. You're not Wonder Woman, you know."

Reassuring Frank that I was fine, I made a teasing comment about his own super powers. And that was all it took for him to get crazy on me. Raising both arms in a Kung Fu position, Frank let out a shrill Bruce Lee war cry. Feigning danger, I laughed as Frank released another high-pitched cry that made him sound more like Tarzan's Chita than a Kung Fu warrior.

The next day, I decided to drive to Tyrone's apartment as soon as I had finished with my last client. After several knocks, the door was opened by a tall teenage girl with coffee-colored skin who had to be Tyrone's sister. "I'm Dr. Martínez," I said, and I held out my hand.

She flashed me a wide smile, revealing a set of perfect ivory teeth. "I'm Zakiya, Celia's friend. She told me all about you."

"All nice things, I hope."

Zakiya grinned, inviting me into the living room where I picked a comfortable spot on the couch. The young boy seated on the matching armchair smiled up at me from the comic book he was reading.

"That's Jerome, the baby of the family," Zakiya explained.

After I said hello to Jerome, I asked if their mother was home, but Zakiya shook her head. "She works the night shift at General Hospital."

I was about to ask for Tyrone when the front door opened, and Tyrone entered the living room. The instant he saw me, his mood darkened. "What are you doing here?" he rudely asked.

"Ty, don't be that way!" Zakiya chastised her older brother who completely ignored his sister's advice.

"I was hoping we could talk for a few minutes." I noticed that Jerome was watching us intently.

"Dr. Martínez, if Maya sent you to talk me into going back to Roosevelt, it won't do you any good!" Tyrone exclaimed. Then he turned around, storming out of the room with Jerome following him.

Looking embarrassed, Zakiya said, "Tyrone's been real creepy since Dad left."

On my feet, I quickly explained that it wasn't her fault and promised to return another time.

All the way home, I thought about Tyrone and his refusal to listen. There had to be a way to break through to him, I thought, pulling into my driveway. As I unlocked the front door and went to hang up my jacket, a sudden thought entered my mind. Ray Gutiérrez. Maybe he could help.

I met Ray several months ago at a workshop he conducted on the new Teen Resource Center in Laguna. It was sponsored by the Equal Opportunity Commission as part of the Male Voices Project. According to Ray, the primary objective of the Male Voices Project was to provide guidance and support for young males, especially for those at-risk.

That's it, I smiled triumphantly as I went into my office to search for Ray's number. After several futile calls, I located the Teen Resource Center, and I was delighted when Ray Gutiérrez answered the phone. "I'm not sure if you remember me," I began cautiously, "but we met several months ago. My name is Sandra Martínez. I'm a psychologist."

"Of course, I remember you," Ray said. "I've heard of all the great things you've done to help our kids."

Thanking Ray, I took a few minutes to praise him for his own accomplishments with at-risk youth. Then I brought up my reason for calling, going into detail about Tyrone's family situation and his decision to drop out of high school. "I tried talking with him today," I continued, "but Tyrone refuses to listen. So I was wondering if maybe you could help."

Ray did not even hesitate for a moment before answering. "Sure, I'd be glad to give it a try, though sometimes it's very tough to break through to the guys. But as you know, here at the Male Voices Project, we're very involved in mentoring young males, especially Chicanos and African

Americans. We help them stay in school and try to teach them how to become responsible young men. Why don't you bring Tyrone by the center tomorrow so we can meet and I can show him around?"

"That would be splendid, Ray. I'm not sure how Tyrone will react, but I promise to get him there, even if I have to bribe him!"

Ray chuckled, adding, "With these guys, sometimes that's what it takes."

Seven

Dr. Martínez

Tyrone's mouth dropped when he found me waiting near the front entrance at Inboxes. "What are you doing here?" he asked miserably. "I thought I made it clear yesterday. I don't need your help."

I was fully prepared for Tyrone's resistence. Despite my petite five-foot-two frame, I had acquired a shrewd reputation in Laguna for taking on anyone and everyone from insensitive school boards to difficult clients. Tyrone was simply of the many troubled teens I had helped over the years. All he really needed was someone to hold his hand and guide him through the harsh winter storm.

"Tyrone, I'm here because I'd like to invite you to meet a friend of mine. All I need is one hour of your time."

Relaxing his lean six-foot frame, Tyrone sighed, "I don't mean to sound rude, Dr. Martínez, but I have to work."

"I spoke with Mr. Morton, your manager, and he's agreed to let you off an hour early today."

Annoyed, Tyrone scowled. "Oh, yeah? Why would I want to do that?"

"Please. There's someone special I'd like you to meet. What's one hour of your time anyway? I promise to drive you home when the hour's up."

Tyrone hesitated, his brooding eyes resting on me for a moment or two before saying, "I'm starved. Can I get a cheeseburger and Coke out of this?"

"Might even splurge on a Big Mac," I answered with a smile of relief as he left to notify the manager.

Several minutes later, we were in my car headed for the south side of Laguna. Tapping his long slender fingers on the dashboard as if he were playing a keyboard, Tyrone asked, "So, who is this person you want me to meet?"

"His name is Ray Gutiérrez. He's a friend of mine who works as the coordinator of the Teen Resource Center that recently opened here in town. Ray's invited us to drop by so you can meet him and see what goes on there."

"So what is this Ray guy supposed to do? Talk me into going back to Roosevelt? Well, it ain't gonna work."

Returning Tyrone's stubborn glare, I calmly replied, "Tyrone, I only want you to meet him. That's all. Ray is a kind human being who devotes all his energy to helping others. You'll like him."

Tyrone muttered something under his breath, but it didn't matter because in my heart I knew that if anyone could get Tyrone to think differently about school, it was Ray. Interrupting Tyrone's moody silence, I decided to share Ray's life story with him in the hopes that it would inspire him as he had done for the audience that day at the workshop. "You know, Tyrone, Ray dropped out of school at the age of fifteen when he got heavily involved with drugs and gangs, and it wasn't until he saw his best friend get killed right in front of him that he realized he didn't want to end up like that. Right then and there, Ray made up his mind to get clean. He dried out with the help of a former teacher, got his G.E.D., and then worked part-time until he completed his university degree."

Tyrone hissed. "Sounds like some kind of sob story. Am I supposed to cry or what?"

"No, of course not," I admitted. "I only want you to know how much Ray cares about himself and others. That's all."

Tyrone didn't make any more wisecracks after that. He remained sulky, tapping away beats on the dashboard as we drove to the south side of the city. We continued past rows of car dealerships and gas stations until we came to a busy intersection where I turned the car into a small shopping center.

"There it is," I exclaimed, noticing the bright yellow sign on the door that read MALE VOICES PROJECT.

"This place is sure ugly," Tyrone said as I parked.

The Teen Resource Center was housed in an old office building. It was sandwiched between Freddy's Food Mart and a vacuum repair shop. There were several other businesses nearby, but they seemed as empty as the rest of the shopping center.

Ignoring Tyrone's snide comment, I led the way to the entrance. Inside, we were instantly greeted by Santana's cat-like guitar sounds, which resonated through the expansive, brightly decorated room. There was a medium-sized pool table to my right, and on the wall directly behind it hung an impressive Aztec calendar. Glancing to my left, I noticed the small room behind the glass window that had to be Ray's office since it had a large desk and filing cabinet.

Ray was standing at the back of the room surrounded by a group of teenage boys, but as soon as he spotted us, he came over to meet us. "Glad you could make it," Ray said, giving me a brief hug. Then, smiling at Tyrone, he held out his hand, saying, "You must be Tyrone." As they shook hands, Tyrone scrutinized Ray's rustic Indian features and the long braid of silvery hair that hung down his blue levi shirt.

"Let me introduce you to some of the guys that are here today," Ray offered. We eagerly followed him to the far side of the room to where a stocky dark-haired Chicano was seated on an armchair that looked twice his size.

Looking up at Tyrone from his math worksheets, the young man squinted his brown eyes, saying, "Hey, I know you. You go to Roosevelt."

Tyrone nodded as Ray introduced Willie Rivera and asked him if he needed any assistance.

"*Chale*, Mr. Gutiérrez," Willie grinned, revealing a set of pointy yellow teeth. "I'm getting the hang of it."

As we moved toward the center of the room, Ray explained, "Willie had dropped out of school a year ago. Now he's working hard to get his G.E.D. He's the oldest student we have, but he's determined to make it."

Pausing next to a guy sitting in a grimy, plaid love seat, Ray said, "This is Kareem." Kareem smiled shyly as Ray explained, "He recently moved from Oakland to Laguna. He's in the ninth grade."

Directing us toward the two students sitting on the couch eating, Ray paused, saying, "These two hungry guys are Kiko and Edgar."

"What's up?" Kiko remarked. His English had a Spanish accent that reminded me of my first encounter with Juanita Chavez's parents. Edgar smiled at us, his wide mouth filled with Doritos.

"Edgar is one of our peer leaders," Ray stated as Kiko gave Edgar a friendly jab in the ribs.

"What's a peer leader?" I asked, noticing that Tyrone seemed to be enjoying the playful banter between Kiko and Edgar.

Ray described the role of the peer leaders, who were selected to represent the MVP at a variety of functions where they were asked to describe the program.

"Some of the criteria we use for selection is attendance and commitment to improving their schoolwork."

"Very impressive," I commented as we followed Ray back toward the entrance.

Pausing in front of a small bulletin board, Ray began to read in his distinct, resonant voice the philosophy of the Male Voices Project: "Male Voices Project participants are honorable young men who respect themselves, others, and the community they live in. By living these principles, MVP holds each other to high standards of conduct and achievement."

After Ray finished, a curly-haired boy, who looked younger than Tyrone's brother, hurried through the front door. Waving some papers in the air at Ray, he demanded, "Mr. Gutiérrez, I need help with these math problems."

"Marcos, I'm busy right now. Ask one of the guys."

Turning to Tyrone, who was watching him closely, Marcos asked, "Can you help me?"

Shrugging his shoulders slightly, Tyrone answered, "Yeah, I guess so."

Marcos smiled, grabbing Tyrone by the arm and leading him across the room to an empty table.

As I followed Ray into his office, he said, "That's Marcos. He's our youngest student."

"Seems like a sweet little guy," I commented, watching Ray clear off a pile of books and papers from the chair next to his desk.

As I sat down, Ray handed me a brochure from another pile on his desk, explaining that the boys, who ranged from ages twelve to sixteen, attended the center every day after school until it closed at 5:30. "I pick them up every day after school in my van, then I take them home at 5:30," he added.

When I asked about their family situations, Ray indicated that all of his students were from low-economic backgrounds. Then he went on to discuss their special needs and the fact that many of these boys were trying hard to stick it out in school despite all of the peer pressures they faced.

After a short while, Tyrone reappeared and Ray promptly thanked Tyrone. "Marcos is the youngest kid here. He's only in sixth grade, and we're struggling to keep him in school."

"Why?" Tyrone asked. I imagined he was thinking about Jerome and how much he depended on Tyrone to help him on a daily basis.

"Well, for one thing, Marcos's dad is gone, so he lives with his mom and younger sister in a hotel."

"In a hotel?" I gasped, my eyes meeting Tyrone's for a brief moment.

Ray nodded.

"How awful," I mumbled, noticing the sadness in Tyrone's eyes.

"But we do our very best to provide positive male role models for the boys who come here," Ray emphasized.

Then he looked directly at Tyrone, saying, "Tyrone, I understand you're not in school anymore. I was wondering if you might like to come here, maybe give me some help with the guys like you did with Marcos."

There was an awkward silence before Tyrone finally answered, "I can't. I have to work."

But Ray was persistent. "Maybe you could come here for a few hours each week." Then he reached inside a drawer for an application form, handing it to Tyrone. "Here's the participation form. Think about what I've said. Maybe show it to your mom. See what she thinks."

Later, as we pulled up to the drive-thru at McDonald's, I asked Tyrone what he had thought of Ray, and he immediately answered, "He's cool."

Tempted to pry something more specific out of Tyrone, I concluded that it was best to give him time to reflect on our visit to the Teen Center.

Eight

Tyrone

The next day, while I'm stacking supplies on the shelves at Inboxes, I think about what Ray Gutiérrez said, that maybe I could help out at the Teen Center. Then, just like that, Marcos pops into my head, and I wonder if I should go back to help the little guy out. The other students seemed nice enough, especially Kareem, but I'm not sure about anything anymore. Got to keep busy working.

When Maya calls me on her cell phone at lunch, I tell her about Dr. Martínez and our visit to the Teen Resource Center.

"Ty, maybe you can talk to the manager, get off early one day out of the week." That's Maya, all right. She always has a plan.

I don't say yes or no to Maya, but all afternoon, I think about her suggestion. Maybe a few hours at the center wouldn't be so bad.

On Saturday, Momma's day off, as soon as I get home from work, she questions me about the participation form Ray gave me. "Son, I found this on the floor in your room. What's it for?"

"Nothing," I answer nonchalantly. But Momma stares me down like a drill sergeant until I'm pressured into telling her about going with Dr. Martínez to the Teen Resource Center.

Momma's face brightens. "It sounds like a good place. You know, what your dad and I always wanted most was for our children to get an education, to get more from life than we did."

"I don't wanna hear about him," I growl.

The somber look returns to Momma's face. "You know it broke my heart when you up and quit going to school. This might be the way back."

"Momma, I don't know if I want to go to the Teen Center. And, besides, you know I need to come home right after work so I can help Jerome with his homework. Zakiya lives on the phone."

Momma puts her hand on my shoulder. "You don't have to worry no more. On Monday, I start working the early morning shift, and I'll be home every day by three o'clock."

Now Momma's face is full of hope, and I can almost hear her reciting verses from Paul Laurence Dunbar, as she continues to plead, "Promise me you'll think about going there."

"Okay, Momma," I reluctantly promise as she reaches out to hug me.

On Monday morning, I approach Mr. Morton, and he agrees to let me off early twice a week so that I can go to the Teen Center. "I think it's a very good idea," he advises. "I dropped out of high school my junior year, but I completed my G.E.D. later."

I listen patiently while Mr. Morton talks about attending the local junior college so he could complete an associate's degree. I finally excuse myself. I feel a bit more hopeful about my own future as I help a customer who is looking for a large mailing tube.

That evening, I call Ray Gutiérrez to let him know about my decision. "You won't regret it," Ray happily says. Then he offers to come by for me in the van when he picks up the other students, but I explain that Maya can take me on her way home from school. Before we hang up, Ray reminds me to have one of my parents sign the participation form.

When Maya drops me off on Tuesday at the Teen Center, I act as if I'm not nervous, even though I feel a little scared. As soon as I walk inside, Ray signals me into his office.

"Hey, bro," Kareem says.

Ray hands each of us a box filled with small cartons of fruit juices. Carrying them to the pool table, we pass them around and quickly find a place to crash on the couch or on one of the chairs scattered throughout the room.

I notice that Marcos is absent as Ray moves to my side, introducing me to the two unfamiliar Chicanos named Jimmy and Lalo.

Grinning proudly, Lalo tells me they're from the continuation school, and Jimmy, who hasn't stopped staring at me, says, "Only the coolest *vatos* go there."

Ray laughs at Jimmy's arrogance while Kiko says, "Yeah, petty thieves go there."

Jimmy says, "Shut up."

Ray quiets them both down with a long hard stare. Then he asks, "Kiko and Edgar, where are your progress reports?"

Smiling, Kiko hands him a folded piece of paper, saying, "I'm passing all my classes."

"*Órale*, me too," Edgar says, handing Ray his progress report.

After Ray compliments them both on bringing up their grades, he turns to me and says, "You know, Jimmy could use some help with his math. Think you can do that?"

"Yeah, *ése*," Jimmy agrees.

"My math grade ain't so hot, but I'll try," I say, moving closer to Jimmy, who pulls out his math homework. I'm shocked to find out it's simple multiplication, but I don't say anything about it as I watch Jimmy struggle with the problems.

At 4:15, Ray directs everyone to the center of the room, explaining to me that once a week they have a Círculo in which they discuss different themes.

When he informs the group that today's topic is respect, a couple of the guys snicker, but Ray calmly states, "See, that's what I'm talking about: being respectful when someone else is talking."

"Listen up, dummies!" Kareem shouts, and the room grows silent.

Ray begins, "What does the word 'respect' mean to each of you?"

Kiko is the first to speak. "It's like when you know someone sees you for who you are, like they really care for you."

"Hey, man, I care for you," Edgar teases his best friend.

Ray asks Edgar, "What does respect mean to you?"

Edgar frowns, "Well, I know it ain't like the way they treat us at school, like we're all gangbangers or dope dealers."

"Who treats you like that?" Ray asks.

Jimmy sneers. "It's all the teachers and administrators."

"Well, what can you do to change that perception?" Ray asks matter-of-factly.

Kiko straightens out his bony shoulders, saying, "Prove them wrong. Show them we're smart, too."

In a pensive mood, Edgar offers, "Do good in school. Turn in our homework. Show them they're wrong."

Nodding, Ray says, "That's right. If you're doing well in school, you're respecting yourself. You're feeling good about yourself, and it'll rub off on those around you. But respect is also something you show others. Like respecting your elders, for example."

"I don't know about that," Jimmy says. "My ol' man didn't respect us; he walked out on our *familia*."

"Yeah, mine too," Kareem says.

Uncomfortable with the discussion, I stare at my dirty sneakers, knowing exactly how it feels when your dad leaves.

"But you can't let that stop you from being successful, from setting goals," Kareem argues, a glint in his dark eyes.

"Yeah, that's true. My ol' man's a drunk, but I ain't gonna be like him," Jimmy says.

"That's right," Ray says. "But respect is also about the way you treat girls."

"I don't know about that," Lalo grins mischievously.

Ray singles me out, asking, "What do you think of respecting girls?"

Thinking back to how mean I acted with Maya when Dad left, lying and cheating on her, I slowly reply, "Yeah, it's important."

Then Lalo brings up his ex-girlfriend, "She was mean . . . dissing me all the time."

When Jimmy joins in, bad-mouthing one of his old girl-friends, Ray is quick to redirect the discussion to the basic definition of respect.

At the end of the session, Ray makes everyone shake hands, saying it's a tradition in the Native American sweat lodges that symbolizes brotherhood. I kind of like shaking hands and even though some of the younger guys giggle, I know they liked it too.

I get a ride home with Ray, who lets me sit with him in the front seat of the van. When Edgar complains, Ray insists I have seniority since I'm the oldest in the group. Kareem didn't come with us because he lives near the center.

Jimmy taps me triumphantly on the shoulder, saying, "*Órale, buey.*"

First, we drop off Jimmy and Lalo who live on the outskirts of Laguna. Then we drive downtown toward the train station, leaving Edgar and Kiko at their apartment building. As soon as we're alone, I ask Ray about Marcos.

He sighs. "Some days he doesn't come. Maybe he'll come more now if he knows you're gonna be helping out."

When we finally arrive at my apartment, I thank Ray, and he smiles, saying, "No problem, Tyrone. I'm very glad you came."

"Yeah, me too," I answer, closing the door behind me.

At dinner, Zakiya, who is in the best of moods since she no longer has to cook, asks, "How was it at the Teen Center?"

"It was good," I tell her.

Jerome asks, "Are you going back again?"

I answer, "Yeah, maybe."

My eyes meet Momma's, and she smiles at me, her face brightening like a California sunset.

Nine

Going to the Teen Center it's not as bad as I thought. Ray's cool, and he never talks down to any of the guys. In the Círculos, he's always giving advice like when he asks one of the guys what his dad would do in a certain situation and the guy says he doesn't have a dad, Ray doesn't give up.

He asks what the guy's grandfather would do and if a guy says his grandpa's no good or he doesn't have one, Ray still tries to get his point across by referring to the ancient Native American ancestors.

Maya thinks that's cool because she's into all that Indian stuff. I just like that Ray knows so much. He says it's from all the books he reads. I also like that Ray goes out of his way to include us in his life. At the end of the day on Fridays, Ray always invites everyone to his Aztec drumming class. I haven't gone yet. Some of the guys went, and they say it's tight.

Lalo's even learning to play the flute. He carries it around with him like it's the most valuable thing he owns.

But helping Marcos is what I enjoy the most. Once he found out I was coming, he started showing up regularly at the Teen Center. He follows me around constantly, like Jerome, and asks me a thousand questions. Marcos is a real smart kid, but I imagine he's embarrassed because he lives in a motel. Must be hard for him to go home every day. Makes our cramped apartment seem like a castle.

Tuesday afternoon, I'm shooting pool with Edgar when a distinguished-looking Black man wearing an expensive suit walks into the Teen Center. Something about the tall stranger seems vaguely familiar, like I've seen him before.

"Man, check out those shoes," Willie says, cradling his cue stick as we watch the visitor go into Ray's office.

Several minutes later, he reappears with Ray, who waves his hands at us that it's time for our Círculo. Once we're all gathered in a circle, Ray says, "This is our guest speaker, Dr. Donald Fife. He's a physician here in Laguna, and today he's going to talk to you about his background and how he became a doctor."

As Dr. Fife clears his voice to speak, I realize he has the same last name as Ankiza. Must be her dad, I think, remembering that her dad's a doctor. It's gotta be him, I tell myself.

"Thank you, Ray. I'm here to share my message with each of you, to tell you that education is the key to success. Each one of you in this room can become anything you want to be with a solid education. It may sound corny, but it's true. You can become a physician, an engineer, a teacher, whatever it is you desire."

Kiko says, "*Órale.*"

Dr. Fife pauses to smile at him before continuing with his speech. "I want you to know that I don't come from a wealthy family. On the contrary, I come from an impover-ished background. My parents are uneducated. My dad only went to the seventh grade, and my mother barely graduated from high school. We lived in southern California, in the Watts area."

"Ain't that the ghetto?" Kareem blurts out.

Dr. Fife nods. "My parents always encouraged me to stay in school, to stay away from gangs and drugs so that I could achieve success. I saw a lot of my friends go down, got caught up in the violence that surrounded us. Nonetheless, I always swore to myself that I would become somebody, that I would get out of the ghetto, and do something with my life."

Willie, who is listening intently to every word Dr. Fife has said, interrupts to say, "That's what I'm gonna do!"

Ray gives Willie a confident pat on the back.

Kareem asks Dr. Fife, "How did you get out of the ghetto?"

"It wasn't easy," Dr. Fife admits. "It took an enormous amount of inner strength. But no one does anything alone. There were significant people along the way, people who believed in me 100 percent. They helped me obtain my first scholarship, which made it possible for me to enter the university. From there, I went on to receive financial aid to study medicine at UCLA."

Ray comments, "Dr. Fife is telling it to you straight. It's all about education. An education gives you the opportunity to succeed both economically and spiritually. It allows you to feel good about yourself and to make positive changes."

Kareem and I exchange a glance as Dr. Fife emphasizes the positive rewards he has received from helping people and for being the first person in his family to become a doctor. Dr. Fife finishes by inviting us to come by his office or to call him if we ever have any questions.

While he passes out his business card to everyone, Ray thanks Dr. Fife, asking us to give him a round of applause. The room instantly fills with whistles and cheers.

I wait until all the guys have left his side, and then I approach Dr. Fife, asking, "Aren't you Ankiza's dad?"

Dr. Fife scrutinizes me with his obsidian eyes. "Yes. Are you a friend of hers?"

"Sort of. I'm Maya's boyfriend, Tyrone."

"Oh, yes. Ankiza's mentioned you. Maya's a nice girl. This is graduation year for all of you. You must be excited. I know Ankiza is."

"Yeah, I guess so," I mumble. Then, before Dr. Fife has time to make any more comments about graduation, I excuse myself, hurrying toward Marcos and Kareem who are signaling for help. Several minutes later, I catch a glimpse of Dr. Fife heading toward the front door.

"He was cool," Kareem says.

I wonder what it would be like to have a Dad like Dr. Fife. Not some loser like my dad.

Momma is talking on the telephone when I get home. "He just walked in," she says, handing me the receiver. "Son, it's your dad. He wants to talk with you."

Uncontrollable anger surges through my body, and I cuss under my breath. Glaring fiercely at Momma, I hurry past her to the stairway. Upstairs in my room, I slam the door shut and go straight to my bed, turning the stereo on as loudly as possible in order to drown out my thoughts. I'm still fuming at the thought of hearing Dad's hypocritical voice, when there are several taps on the door and Momma slowly walks inside.

"Your dad wants to come home."

Noticing the softness in Momma's voice, I ask, "You told him no, didn't you?"

Momma takes a deep breath and lowers her eyes, and I can't help but grunt in displeasure.

Momma is quickly at my side, sinking her tired body onto the edge of the bed. Now there are tears in her eyes.

"Your dad, he's a good man."

"Then why'd he leave us like that?"

Momma is speechless for a few moments. She wipes away a stray tear streaming down her face.

"Momma, please don't cry," I attempt to console her, touching her stooped shoulder. "I didn't mean to make you cry."

Momma's teary eyes search me out. "It's not your fault. But I want you to listen carefully to what I'm about to say. I want to tell you about your dad, how hard it was for him growing up without a father."

"Does that give him the right to leave?" I cry accusingly.

Shaking her head, Momma says, "You know your dad grew up in South Central. There were six of them. His father left when he was only four, so his Momma was the one that had to keep the family together. They were so poor. Sometimes they went without eating. Your dad said his momma wouldn't let them eat until she gave them a laxative because they hadn't eaten for so long, she was afraid they'd be constipated. Your dad grew up on the streets. It's by the grace of God that he survived."

"So what? You grew up poor, too, but you never left us," I answer adamantly.

Momma pauses, taking a long deep breath before she continues. "I'm not trying to make excuses for your dad, but there's something that happens with poverty and racism. It eats away at a Black man's soul, at his pride. Sometimes it's easier for men to leave because they feel they don't have nothing tying them down. They follow the same pattern their father followed. Your dad told me he never heard anyone in his family talk about their fathers. He never even knew where his father was or why he left."

"So that excuses him? Because his father did it, he can do it, too?"

"No, of course not, and that's why your dad wants to come home. He told me he's been going to AA and that he left because he knew he needed to get straight. Now he just needs another chance. Won't you give it to him?"

I look away from Momma's pleading eyes toward the Lakers' poster Jerome made when he was in third grade. There's a picture of Kobe Bryant in the middle, and he's surrounded by purple and gold stars. If only life were like basketball, perfect like Kobe Bryant's dunks, I think to myself.

Momma rises to her feet, whispering sadly, "Please think about what I said."

After Momma leaves, I think about what she said about Dad's life. Then I think of how Dr. Fife said he was also poor when he was young. Why couldn't Dad have done something positive like Dr. Fife? Why couldn't he have made his family proud instead of tearing us all apart?

Ten

Wednesday evening, we're almost finished with dinner when the doorbell rings. Jerome hurries off to answer it, and moments later, he reappears in the kitchen with Dr. Martínez, who is apologetic for not calling first. Rising from the table, Momma invites the unexpected guest to try some of her tuna casserole.

Dr. Martínez politely refuses, "My husband, Frank, is cooking his famous spaghetti tonight, and I can't let him down."

"That's the kind of husband I want one day," Zakiya states, giving me a smug glance. "One who can cook."

Dr. Martínez smiles when Jerome proudly adds, "My dad can cook hamburgers."

I'm about to walk out of the kitchen, when Dr. Martínez says, "Wait, Tyrone. I wanted to talk with both you and your mom."

Taking the hint, Zakiya orders Jerome to help her with the dishes. I reluctantly follow Momma and Dr. Martínez into the living room.

They strike up a conversation about Momma's new job at the hospital. Momma eagerly talks about her switch to daytime hours and how relieved she is to be home by the time Jerome gets out of school.

Then Dr. Martínez turns to me and says, "It must be nice, having your mom home in the evenings."

"It's okay," I answer, still wondering why Dr. Martínez is here.

As if she has read my thoughts, Dr. Martínez says, "Tyrone, I talked to Mr. Grinde. He informed me that it's still not too late for you to return to Roosevelt. He believes there's time for you to make up all the work you've missed so that you can graduate with your class. What do you think?"

Momma's eyes shimmer with excitement. "Dr. Martínez, I want you to know that I never wanted Tyrone to drop out. It would make me so happy if Tyrone went back to school and graduated with his class."

My voice hardening, I cry out, "That's for me to decide! Besides, I have to work now. You know we need the money badly."

Dr. Martínez remains calm despite the tension in the air. "Maybe you can work after school and on weekends."

Shaking my head, I wonder why we're even having this conversation.

Momma pleads with me again, "Please listen to me. If it's about the money, I can clean houses on weekends."

"Stay out of this, Momma!" I shout back at her, realizing I've hurt Momma's feelings again. I whisper a cuss word.

Momma glares at me, saying, "Don't you talk back, you hear me?" She excuses herself and then goes into the kitchen to help Zakiya and Jerome.

Dr. Martínez says, "She only wants the best for you."

"Yeah, I know, but sometimes Momma pushes too much."

Nodding as if she understands, Dr. Martínez asks me, "How's the Teen Resource Center?"

Pushing my guilty thoughts away, I eagerly begin to describe the new friends I've made. "And remember that young kid, Marcos? He never leaves my side. Sometimes I think he invents homework just so I can help him."

"How sweet," Dr. Martínez smiles. "I understand that Ankiza's dad was a guest speaker?"

Slightly irritated that Dr. Martínez has been checking up on me, I answer, "Yeah, he's tight." All of a sudden, I can hear Dr. Fife's voice resonating loudly and clearly in my mind: *Education is the key to success.*

"I'm glad you liked Ankiza's dad," Dr. Martínez says. "He's worked very hard to get where he is, just like Ray Gutiérrez." Then, glancing quickly at her watch, Dr. Martínez adds, "I have to get home now, but please think about going back to school. Also, I'd like to meet with you in my office once a week, if possible."

"And why would I want to do that?" I retort as Momma reappears in the living room.

Overhearing Dr. Martínez, Momma warns, "Watch your mouth." Then she turns to Dr. Martínez and says, "That's real nice of you. But we don't have no money to pay for that."

"Don't worry about the money," Dr. Martínez says, her eyes twinkling. "It won't cost anything. Well, maybe Tyrone will have to buy me a Pepsi every now and then."

Then she winks at Momma as if I've already accepted her offer.

Driving home with Ray the following evening, I tell him what Dr. Martínez said about being able to return to Roosevelt. "I think it would be a smart idea to go back. That way, you could still graduate and go to college," Ray advises. "You know, Tyrone, it's never too late. I'm the living example of that."

I don't contradict Ray. Instead, I listen attentively as he talks about how difficult it was when he finally made the decision to get his G.E.D. and go to college in Bakersfield where he was living. "A day doesn't pass that I am not grateful for my decision," he says. "I might still be on the streets or, even worse, dead, if it hadn't been for my education."

As much as I try, I can't imagine Ray as a gangbanger. He seems so together, as if he's always been that way.

We're passing the grocery store where Dad used to work, so I point it out to Ray. Then I sarcastically mimic Dad's voice on the phone the other night and how he's begging Momma to come home.

"And why does that bother you?" Ray asks me point-blank.

"I think he should stay the hell away. He doesn't fool me by saying that he's changed and that he's not a drunk anymore."

Ray frowns, "You know, people do change. Maybe you oughta give your dad another chance."

"He doesn't deserve it," I answer defensively, but Ray doesn't pursue the subject any further. Instead, we talk about hip-hop music and the latest reggaeton craze that's hit Laguna. When we pull up to my apartment, Ray advises me to think carefully about returning to Roosevelt.

Maya calls after dinner that night, and when I tell her about Dr. Martínez's visit, Maya gets crazy on me, begging me to think seriously about the possibility of going back to school. I don't know how Maya does it, but by the time we hang up, I've promised to call Mr. Grinde.

The next morning, I call Mr. Grinde during my lunch break, and he convinces me to give it a try, insisting, like Ray, that it's never too late. Hesitating, I agree to return, pointing out that I need to finish out the week at Inboxes. That same afternoon, I talk to Mr. Morton, and he happily agrees to change my work schedule to evenings and weekends.

The following Monday, I'm back on campus, and before Maya goes to her first period class, she walks me to the counseling offices. Mr. Grinde, who is very pleased to see me, takes me into his office, and we review the notes from all of my teachers on my missing assignments. Then Mr. Grinde writes me a tardy slip, and with knots forming in my stomach, I hurry to my algebra class.

All eyes are on me as I hand Mr. B. my tardy slip.

"Glad to have you back," he says. "We're reviewing Chapter Seven for the upcoming test."

As I make my way down the aisle to my old seat, I notice that Jonathan's seat is empty, but I could care less since I don't plan on getting into any more fights. Opening my binder, I start to copy the problem that Mr. B. is working on the board, but I don't get a chance to finish it before the bell rings.

Tonya, the class brain, welcomes me back as I walk out into the hallway with Tommy.

"Maya said you were coming back. That's cool. Listen, if you need any help with Mr. B.'s assignment, let me know."

"Thanks," I answer. Tommy goes off in the opposite direction. As I exit the building, I wonder what I would do without good friends like Tommy and Rudy.

By noon, I'm slightly overwhelmed by all the homework I've accumulated, but I shake it off the minute I see Maya standing in front of my locker.

"Hey, babe," I say, slipping my arm around her skinny waist and stealing a kiss.

"How were your classes?" Maya asks.

"Not bad," I answer taking my lunch out of my locker.

"Cool. Everyone's waiting at the bleachers. They're excited you're back."

We're walking past the gym when we come face to face with Mickey and two other girls. Maya reaches out for my hand and gives Mickey the coldest stare. But Mickey only glares back at Maya as she walks right past us with her two friends.

"What a ho," Maya mutters, reminding me I better not even glance at Mickey, let alone talk to her.

At the bleachers, Sheena is the first to ask how my classes went. "Real tight, but I have a lot of makeup work."

Maya eagerly replies, "Don't worry, Ty. We can all help you."

Ankiza and Rina both nod in agreement while Rudy says, "Yeah, Juanita will help you!"

Juanita pinches Rudy on the arm, saying, "What about you, *flojo?*"

That's all Rina needs to get started. Taunting Rudy about his C+ in P.E., Rina engages Rudy in a verbal match that keeps getting louder.

Rudy finally jumps off the bleachers and raises his fists playfully in the air, saying, "Come on, Rina Schwarzennegger!"

By now, we're all laughing as Rina replies, "Rudy, you couldn't hurt a *mosca!*"

After school, I get a ride to Inboxes and by the time I finally get home, it's almost seven o'clock. Momma meets me at the door, saying, "I'm so proud of you. Zakiya told me you went back to school today."

There are tears in Momma's eyes, but this time they're tears of joy as she reaches over to embrace me.

Jerome, who is right behind her, grins like a Cheshire cat. He asks, "Will you help me with my social studies homework?"

Zakiya, who is on the couch watching TV, yells out, "Don't ask him, Jerome. I'm the smartest one in the family!"

"That's right, baby. You're smart like your momma," Momma says. Then she calls me into the kitchen so I can have some of her pot roast.

When Jerome says that he's still hungry, Momma and I exchange another happy smile.

Eleven

Dr. Martínez

It took almost a week of coaxing to get Tyrone into my office. At first, he resisted strongly, but with Maya and Juanita's help, he finally agreed.

His long legs awkwardly sticking out of my leather couch, Tyrone's eyes darted around the room until they finally rested on the Lakers' calendar near my desk. "Are you a Lakers fan?" he asked timidly.

"I never was until I married Frank. Now we watch every single game together. He's a Lakers fanatic."

"Yeah, me too. Jerome and I never miss a game."

"Have you ever gone to the Staples Center?" I pried, noticing that Tyrone's jaw muscles were more relaxed.

Tyrone's eyes dimmed as he nodded, "Once, with my dad."

As Tyrone fell silent, I waited calmly for him to break the silence.

After a very long minute, he leaned back, saying. "I really like my work at the Teen Center."

"That's great. Is Marcos still following you around?"

"Yeah, he acts like Jerome."

"My brother Andy used to do that."

Now Tyrone's brooding eyes focused intently on me. "You have a brother?"

"Yes, but he died very young," I admitted as painful memories of Andy's death emerged from the neat little box where I'd stored them all these years. "How does it feel being back in school?" I continued, focusing my attention back on Tyrone.

"Good. My teachers have been cool, but I still have a lot of work to make up."

"I'm sure Maya will help," I offered, watching a shy smile spread across Tyrone's smooth face.

"Yeah, Maya and Tommy have both been helping me with my algebra."

"They sound like terrific friends."

"Yeah, I guess so."

"How are things at home with your mom? She must be pleased now that you're back in school."

Frowning, Tyrone replied, "She's an idiot."

"What makes you say that?"

His back stiffening, Tyrone took a deep breath. "Dad asked if he could move back home, and Momma said yes right away. She's stupid. After he walked out on her, she's taking him back. I hope he never comes home."

"You know, Tyrone, people make mistakes."

"Well, I don't care!" Tyrone stated loud and clear. "I don't need him. I don't even want a dad. Momma's plain ol' stupid, acting like everything's all right, like he didn't betray his wife and kids."

For a brief moment, I thought about what it had been like for Andy and me growing up with a father who was always drunk. It had taken me years to work through the pain, but the scars were still there. Staring into Tyrone's troubled eyes, I said, "Fathers aren't perfect, Tyrone. No one is. My father hurt Andy and me a great deal when we were young."

Tyrone asked, "How did he do that?"

"My dad's been an alcoholic all his life. Ever since I can remember he was drunk. It was almost as if Andy and I never had a father."

"My dad's a drunk, too," Tyrone admitted. "And now he swears to Momma that he's gonna change and that he's going to those AA meetings."

"Tyrone, at least your Dad is trying. My father has always refused to go to AA meetings. My mother's attended them, and I've gone to a few, but not Dad."

"You've gone to AA meetings?" Tyrone asked me in disbelief.

"Yes, I have."

Tyrone looked toward the window as he reflected on what I'd just revealed to him. After a few moments, he turned to me, abruptly stating, "You know what? I've been thinking about it, and I think I really don't want to be an engineer. Maybe I'd like to be a counselor like Ray, you know, and work with kids like Marcos."

"I think that's a splendid idea," I agreed, noting the confidence in Tyrone's voice.

"But I don't know how to go about doing that. I was thinking of talking to Ray about it and finding out how he did it."

"I'm sure Ray can give you some direction, and Laguna University has a reputable degree program in counseling and social work. Why don't you talk to Mr. Grinde about your change in college plans? He'll be able to talk with you about the coursework you'll need."

Nodding, Tyrone rose to his feet. "I gotta go. Maya's supposed to give me a ride to Inboxes."

As I walked Tyrone to the door, I asked if it would be all right to schedule another appointment for him in two weeks, and he agreed without any resistance whatsoever. Patting him on the arm gently, I reminded him, "Think about talking to your dad. People do make mistakes," I repeated as he dashed toward the front entrance.

Frank was at the door waiting for me when I arrived. After a mushy kiss that tasted like garlic and spaghetti sauce, he took my briefcase from me and led me to the couch, saying, "Your mother called from Delano. Your dad's in the hospital."

"Is he all right?" I asked, feeling a slight throbbing around my temples. Frank ran his fingers tenderly through my hair.

"I guess he started to bleed internally, but Mom said he's gonna be okay. They got it to stop."

"Was he drinking again?" I demanded to know, secretly hoping I was wrong. Maybe for once it was something else.

Frank nodded solemnly as he pulled me closer, whispering, "Mom wants you to meet her at the hospital. I tried to tell her you're still recovering from losing the baby, but you know how she is."

My eyes felt wet as I bluntly stated, "I'm damn sick and tired of seeing Dad like that, racing to Delano each time he almost drinks himself to death. Sometimes I wish he'd drop dead!"

"Sandra, you don't mean that," Frank scolded, lifting the edge of his favorite Rolling Stones T-shirt to wipe my teary face. "Mick Jagger's not gonna like this," he warned playfully.

I was suddenly filled with remorse, my thoughts drifted back to my conversation with Tyrone. Alcoholism was a disease. Dad was sick, and he needed help just like Tyrone's father.

Drawing in a deep breath, I whispered, "I guess I can cancel my afternoon appointments and leave at noon."

"Hon," Frank insisted in a gentle soothing voice, "I don't want you going all the way to Delano by yourself. I'll take a half-day so that I can drive you there."

"Are you sure you want to do that?" I asked, nudging my head up against Frank's chest.

Tightening his arms around me, Frank nodded, adding, "Watch out for Mick's lips!"

We both smiled as I drew back from Frank for a moment; smoothed out his T-shirt, and apologized to Mick.

Twelve

Dr. Martínez

After a tedious drive through the dusty San Joaquin Valley, we arrived in Delano, César Chávez's historic agricultural town where I had spent my childhood and adolescent years. Despite the new subdivisions on the outskirts of the city, Delano still epitomized the legacy of the UFW and its humble farmworkers, who, like Steinbeck's migrants in *The Grapes of Wrath*, had survived against all odds. As a teenager, I had hungrily devoured every chapter of Steinbeck's Pulitzer-prize winning novel, reflecting on all the suffering my own family had endured while working in the fields.

I let out a deep sigh as we turned into the hospital, realizing how often I'd been here in the past few years. I was beginning to hate this place. All it did was bring sad memories. Frank reached out to squeeze my hand, and I forced out a smile, suddenly aware that I couldn't have done this without Frank at my side.

"Don't worry, hon," Frank reassured me. "Your mom said he's gonna be fine."

"She's in denial, and we both know it."

"Leave my *suegra* alone," Frank answered playfully, but my sense of humor had evaporated like the morning fog.

In the visiting area, we took the nearest elevator until we found Dad's room on the third floor. The first bed was occupied by a large, middle-aged man who appeared to be asleep despite the small tube running through his nose and around his head to the oxygen tank at his bedside.

As we approached Dad's bed, Mom rose from her chair. Her small eyes were sunken, and her thin graying hair was pulled back in a bun. Embracing Frank, she said, "How are you, *hijo*? Is Sandra feeding you well?"

His blue eyes dancing, Frank patted his round stomach. "Can't you see how much bigger my *panza* is getting?"

Mom chuckled, giving me a hug before I moved to the bed rail to greet Dad, who was opening his eyes. His cheeks were puffy, and his nose seemed redder than usual. There was an IV taped to his right hand that hung limply at his side. I noticed he wasn't wearing his favorite diamond ring that Frank and I had given him last Christmas.

"How are you, Dad?" I asked, kissing him lightly on his spider-veined cheek.

"*Bien, hija*," Dad whispered, his voice faint and raspy.

"His throat is sore from the tube they had to put through his mouth to his stomach to stop the bleeding," Mom explained as Frank moved to my side.

In a solemn voice, Frank asked Dad how he was feeling, and they exchanged a few words.

Unwilling to waste any more time, I demanded, "Dad, why do you keep hurting yourself like this?"

"I told him one of these days he's gonna kill himself," Mom interrupted, her words like a cold bitter winter.

I was tempted to tell Mom to shut up once and for all. My eyes grew blurry as Dad focused his hazel eyes on me. "*Hija,*" he whispered, "this time I'm gonna stop drinking. I promise. I'm gonna try the antabuse again."

I wanted to offer Dad some reassurance, to let him know that I believed every word he was saying, but the words were stuck in my throat. Silence drifted into the room. Dad abruptly asked Frank, "How's income tax season? Keeping you busy?"

Smiling, Frank replied, "You wouldn't believe some of the deductions people try to claim, doggie therapy or kitty play equipment. I'm thinking Sandy and I should get a pet, so we can claim it!"

Dad tried to laugh, but instead he began coughing. I quickly handed him a glass of water from the table at his bedside.

Leaning back against his pillow, Dad asked, "How have you been feeling, *hija*?"

"I'm much better," I answered, anticipating a series of questions about the baby I'd recently lost, but I was saved by the nurse who whisked into the room, announcing it was time to check Dad's vital signs.

Mom said, "It's getting late. Let's go home so I can make dinner. My *compadre* Jesus brought me, so I'll have to ride home with both of you."

"No *problema*," Frank eagerly stated, using the best Spanish he knew, which always seemed to come out wrong.

As I gave Dad a brief kiss on his pale cheek, I promised we'd stop by in the morning before returning to Laguna. Then, waving good-bye, Frank and I followed Mom who was already headed for the corridor.

Driving through the old barrio where I had spent my childhood years, I was flooded with memories of playing kick the can on hot summer evenings with my friends until it grew dark and our parents hollered at us to go inside. As we continued past modest wood-framed houses with large unkempt yards, we came to Don Nacho and Doña Martina's house, where I was greeted by the familiar statue of the Virgin of Guadalupe. Carefully placed in the center of their front yard, the beautiful hand-painted ceramic statue of Mexico's patron saint stood nearly three feet tall. It was surrounded by several yellow and red rosebushes as well as an assortment of colorful potted plants. Two gold plaster angels had been placed at the feet of the stoic brown madonna along with several other statues of saints.

"See the new statue of the Santo Niño de Atocha that my *comadre* found at the flea market," Mom pointed.

I tried to imagine what they were going to do when all their saints no longer fit in their yard. The sacred altar grew with each passing year as Don Nacho and his wife added new saints, making the sacred shrine a landmark in the neighborhood. One Christmas, Mom had mailed me a clipping from the *Delano Times*. Don Nacho's altar had appeared on the front page. It was major news in the barrio.

As we pulled up in front of Mom and Dad's faded yellow house, I noticed that Don Anselmo's 54 Chevy pick up was missing from his front yard. Don Anselmo had been our neighbor since we had first moved into the barrio, and he always parked his pickup in the same spot. When I asked Mom about it, she explained, *"Pobre, Don Anselmo.* He had to give it to his son. *Ya no puede manejar. Casi perdió la vista en un ojo."*

We went in through the back door to the kitchen, and Mom immediately ordered Frank and I into the living room while she began to prepare dinner. When I saw Dad's empty recliner, I felt a heaviness in my heart. Then my eyes darted up to the pictures on the wall, and I was struck by Andy's haunting green eyes staring at me from his sophomore high school picture.

Unable to move, I felt Frank gently pull me toward the bedrooms. "Come on, hon. Let's take a siesta. Mom will call us when dinner's ready."

Moments later, lying next to Frank, who was already drifting off to sleep, all I could think about was Andy and the mysterious car accident that had taken his life. With each passing year, I'd continued to wonder if Andy's death had been a suicide as the police had suspected. It was something we never talked about, ignoring all the unanswered questions. Why was it that our family always avoided the truth as if it were a deadly form of cancer?

I was jolted back to reality when I heard Mom's voice calling out that dinner was ready.

"Wake up, *panzón,*" I told Frank, tapping him on the shoulder until he awoke.

In the kitchen, Mom had placed a platter of neatly rolled enchiladas at the center of the table. *"Hija,* I made these for you," Mom said, her tired eyes shining like gold fields.

Pulling up a chair, Frank sighed, "Oh, Mom, I thought you made the enchiladas for me."

"For you too, *hijo*," Mom said with a smile.

I couldn't help but think about all the ways Mom tried to show me how much she cared, despite the fact that we disagreed on almost everything.

After consuming a record-breaking nine enchiladas, Frank finally set his fork down, insisting that his *panza* couldn't take another bite. When he offered to wash the dishes, Mom frowned, chasing him into the living room to watch TV. According to Mom's outdated beliefs, household work was for women only. Not men. It was no wonder Dad was unable to wash a single plate or even reach across the table for the salt shaker.

Once we were alone, I knew I couldn't withhold my true feelings any longer. "Mom, we both know the antabuse isn't going to work."

Handing me another dish to dry, Mom replied dryly, "We don't know that, Sandra. Maybe your dad will quit this time."

"Why don't you talk to him again about joining AA?"

The dark line on Mom's forehead deepened. "I've tried, *hija*. Your friend Sarah Johnson tried, but he still refuses to go."

"What's wrong with him?" I cried angrily. "Doesn't Dad realize he could die the next time he bleeds?"

Mom drew in a long breath, shaking her head sadly. We both fell into a hopeless silence, unwilling to say anything else that might increase the hurt we had both lived with all these years.

By the time we awakened the next day, Mom had cooked enough *huevos con chorizo* for an entire regiment. As soon as we were finished with breakfast, we gathered up our belongings and drove out to the hospital.

When Frank turned the car into the parking lot, I instructed, "Drop Mom off at the curb."

"Aren't we going in to see Dad?" he asked in astonishment.

"No," I whispered. Frank tried to convince me to change my mind, but I remained adamant, repeating, "No, Frank. I've had it. I can't do this any more."

From the backseat, Mom made a clicking sound of disapproval. "*Ándale, hija. No seas mal agradecida.* You told him last night you were coming this morning."

As the car came to a halt, I turned around and gave Mom a cold stare. "Tell Dad I had an emergency call or something."

Mumbling something under her breath, Mom descended from the car, pausing to embrace Frank, who quietly held the door open for her. As I watched Mom walk slowly toward the entrance, I felt a sharp stab of guilt, but I was tired of all the lies.

Thirteen

Tyrone

Late Saturday afternoon, as the city bus drops me off at the corner, I hurry home feeling exuberant because Mr. Morton complimented me in front of everyone when I went out of my way to help an elderly man carry two large filing boxes out to his car. Momma always taught me to help others, especially old people because one day we're all gonna be old. My good mood instantly disappears when I spot Dad's banged up Plymouth parked in front of our apartment.

"He's back," I mumble to myself, dreading the thought of seeing him, wishing he'd go away like before. As I cross the street, Dad comes walking out the front door with Jerome, who glances nervously from Dad to me.

"Hello, son," Dad says, his razor-sharp eyes scrutinizing me. He's wearing the bright green shirt with palm trees that we bought him for Father's Day.

"I'm not your son!" I shout defensively, rushing past him as he begs me to wait, but the only answer he receives is the banging of the screen door.

Zakiya, who has witnessed the entire scene from the doorway, sneers at me. "You don't have to act so mean with Dad."

Warning her to stay out of my business, I bolt up the stairway to my bedroom before she can make another stupid comment. After I turn the radio on, I reach for my new issue of *URBE* magazine, but I can't concentrate on any of the articles. Dad's face keeps appearing in my head. Why did he have to come back? Why couldn't he forget we exist?

Just then, Momma cracks open the door to say, "Son, I'm making a special dinner for your Dad tonight. Won't you please join us?"

Flinging my magazine across the room, I angrily cry out, "Momma, you know how I feel about Dad coming home."

Moving to my bedside, Momma places her hand tenderly on my shoulder, and I'm reminded of how she used to cradle me in her arms when I was little and afraid that there were monsters in the room. "Please," she begs, her voice cracking.

Now there are tears in Momma's eyes. I hate it when Momma cries because it makes me feel crappy, like a good-for-nothing son.

"All right, I'll do it," I finally answer gruffly.

Her face softening, Momma wipes away a tear, thanking me several times before she leaves the room. Leaning back against my pillow, I can hear Ray saying that everybody deserves a second chance. Not Dad, I mutter to myself. He's nothing but a loser.

An hour later, Jerome comes into the room, announcing, "Dinner's ready. You're coming, aren't you, Tyrone?" he asks in a timid voice.

Reaching for my sneakers, I nod in agreement. Jerome happily says, "Dad said he's gonna take me fishing tomorrow."

"If he's not drunk," I mumble, watching the hopeful look disappear from Jerome's face.

Momma smiles when I walk into the kitchen and pull up a chair next to Zakiya, who is having an animated conversation with Dad about her computer class. It ticks me off that Dad is finally taking an interest in our schoolwork. He never said anything about it before, but now he's acting as if he really cares. Who does he think he's scamming, anyway?

Chewing on a mouthful of Momma's tuna casserole, I try my best to block out their conversation until Dad suddenly turns to me and says, "Son, your momma told me you went back to school and how you're working and all. I'm real proud of you for doing all of that."

Although Dad's eyes are burning holes through me, I refuse to look directly at him. Instead, I continue eating as if I haven't heard a word he's uttered.

In a futile attempt to diffuse the tension that is slowly mounting, Momma remarks "Jerome got all A's and B's on his report card this quarter."

Out of the corner of my eye, I watch Dad reach out to pat Jerome on his curly head.

"Tyrone always makes me do my homework," Jerome proudly says, glancing my way momentarily.

"That's good, son. You wanna be smart like your brother and sister."

"He sure does," Zakiya exclaims.

Dad smiles warmly. "How about if I take everyone to church in the morning after my AA meeting?"

Zakiya says, "Cool, I can see my friends there."

"Can we go to the beach, too?" Jerome asks.

"Sure we can," Dad agrees while Zakiya begins to whine about bringing along one of her friends.

Unwilling to tolerate another second of this idyllic Kodak family scene, I push my chair back, excusing myself.

Momma whispers, "You hardly ate."

Shrugging my shoulders, I turn to leave, but not before I glare at Dad, letting him know that he might've fooled Momma with that AA talk, but he hasn't fooled me one bit.

When Maya picks me up on Sunday, she's surprised to see the apartment empty. On the way to Pizza Hut to meet our friends, I describe Dad's homecoming and our happy family dinner. "I wouldn't even look at him when he talked to me," I say.

"Don't you think you're being too hard on your dad?" Maya asks. "After all, he did come back. My dad never came back. What I wouldn't give if he and my mom had gotten back together." Now there is a wistful expression on Maya's face, and I know she's thinking back to the day her dad left.

"It's way too late," I reply adamantly. "Anyway, I don't need my dad for anything."

Frowning, Maya slows down for the first intersection on Main Street. "Ty, why do you have to be so stubborn?"

"Look who's talking!" I defend myself. Maya flashes me a smile, exposing her perfect white teeth.

We find an empty parking space across from City Hall, and then we head for Pizza Hut, which is one of our favorite downtown hangouts. Strolling hand in hand, Maya pauses along the way to check out the clothes in the fancy store windows. When we come to Victoria's Secret, I'm the one who stops.

Pointing to the sexy pink nightie on the faceless mannequin, I say, "Hey, babe, that's what I'm gonna get you for your birthday."

Yanking me away, Maya says, "How do you know I don't already have one?"

At Pizza Hut, we make our way to the back where Sheena, Tommy, Rudy, and Juanita are seated at a large booth near the bathrooms. As Tommy scoots over to make room for us, Juanita asks about Ankiza, and Maya explains that she had to babysit.

"Where's Rina Schwarzenegger?" I ask.

"She's at work," Rudy says.

"Poor Rina," Sheena comments. "McDonald's is a crappy place to work. But, hey, maybe that's where I need to get a job, so I can save up some money to move out. Mom's ragging on me all the time. I don't know what's up her butt."

"Tell me about it," Tommy agrees. "All my old man does is complain."

I'm about to offer a nasty remark about my own dad when the waitress appears. We quickly add up our money to see if we have enough for two large pizzas. Then, while we wait for our order, Rudy, Tommy, and I go over to play video games. The girls refuse to join us since they think video games are too violent.

Typical chicks, I think to myself as Tommy and I begin a game of Karate Warriors, leaving Rudy alone to play his favorite game, Battlefield Death. We play several rounds until Maya and Juanita finally drag us back to the booth to eat.

After we're done watching Rudy stuff his face with the last slice of pizza, we go back outside to walk around. The instant Maya sees the trolley go by, she insists we take a ride on it. Juanita and Sheena eagerly agree, so we wait on the next street corner until the trolley comes by again. As we jump aboard, several tourists turn to stare at us, but we don't let it get to us since we're used to the looks we get, living in a mostly white city.

After a scenic ride through downtown Laguna, we get off at the nearest ice-cream parlor, where we gather around a table to talk trash and eat ice cream. When Juanita tells Rudy that it's time to take her home so she can finish her book report, we unanimously agree it's time to go hit the books.

As Maya pulls up to the apartment and we kiss good-bye, she whispers, "Ty, try to be nicer to your dad. Remember, he did come back. Some dads never do."

When I walk inside, I find Dad in the living room watching the Lakers game with Zakiya and Jerome.

As soon as he sees me, Dad calls out, "Lakers are up, son. How was your date with Maya?"

Silence is the only answer I give him as I cross toward the stairway. My angry thoughts erase Maya's words of advice.

Fourteen

Tyrone

By the time I come downstairs on Monday morning, Dad's already left to drive Momma to work at the hospital.

As I join Zakiya for a bowl of cereal, she says, "We had fun at the beach."

When I make a grunting noise, Zakiya stares me down with her instrusive obsidian eyes. "Why are you acting like that, Ty? Dad's trying hard, but you think you're too good."

Then Zakiya storms off into the living room to call Jerome, who hollers good-bye to me as they leave for the bus stop. Irritated, I serve myself another bowl of cereal. If anyone thinks they're too good, it's Zakiya. She's always been Dad's prissy little girl, sticking up for him all the time. Not me. I can see right through him.

At the sound of several loud honks, I grab my backpack and hurry outdoors to meet Rudy and Tommy, who are parked across the street.

"What took you so long, *ése*?" Rudy complains as I slide into the backseat.

"Chill out," Tommy says as we pull away from the curb. "Rudy's pissed 'cause his dad wouldn't lend him the car."

"Shut up," Rudy orders Tommy, who cranks up the radio to drown Rudy out.

When we arrive at the campus parking lot, Rudy asks about Maya, whose blue Nissan is parked in the first row. "She and Ankiza have a Peer Helpers' meeting. You know Maya talked Ankiza into joining the group with her. It's part of the peer communications class they took last year."

"Must be a chick thing," Rudy says. "They're always trying to help someone."

Tommy accuses Rudy of making a sexist remark, but Rudy only laughs as Tommy maneuvers his car between a four-wheel-drive truck and a brand-new Mustang.

After we stop at our lockers, Tommy and I hurry to our first period class. We're entering the Math building when we see Mickey. Flicking her eyes at me for an instant, Mickey tightens her hold on the arm of the long-haired dude next to her. She walks straight past me as if she hasn't even seen me.

"What a relief," I tell Tommy, "Looks like Mickey finally got the hint and decided to pounce on someone else."

Grinning, Tommy says, "I think Rina Schwarzenegger scared her!"

The tardy bell rings as we hurry into the classroom. As I move down the aisle to my seat, Mr. B. informs everyone that we're having a pop quiz. Several loud groans fill the air as Mr. B. starts to hand it out to the class. When Jonathan makes an obnoxious snorting sound, I lean forward to tell him to shut his ugly face, but Cal beats me to it. Then

Bethany, who sits next to Jonathan, calls him a perve, so I don't have to do anything. I feel a sense of relief since I wouldn't want to cause any more trouble for Mr. B. He's been cool since I returned to Roosevelt, helping me at lunch with my makeup assignments.

U.S. government turns out worse than Mr. B.'s quiz. Mr. Pollard almost puts us to sleep with his lecture on federal and state income taxes, attempting to explain why all good citizens have to pay Uncle Sam. It's all a scam, I think. The rich get richer off all the tax breaks while the poor get their wages eaten up by taxes. No way is Mr. Pollard gonna convince me that we have a fair tax system.

When Janie raises her hand to ask why we can't be like Canada where they have no taxes and socialized medical care, Mr. Pollard goes off on another long tangent about why Canada's government is inadequate. By then, everyone has tuned him out, even Janie.

During our lunch break, we cram into Maya's car and drive to McDonald's. Ankiza sits in the front with Maya and me while Rudy, Juanita, Rina, and Sheena all squeeze into the backseat. The only one missing is Tommy, who had a meeting with a teacher.

On the way there, Rudy yells at Rina, "Scoot your fat butt over."

Rina pinches him in the arm and says, "At least I ain't puny like you!"

Ankiza shouts at them both. "You guys are behaving worse than my little sister, Athena."

After we pick up our order at the drive-thru window, Maya pulls into the nearest parking space. As Rudy and

Juanita get out of the car to eat, Rina quips, "Now I can eat my burger in peace."

While we're eating, Ankiza mentions the graduation party her mom and dad are planning for her in May.

"Is Hunter gonna be here?" I ask, hoping that the answer is yes, since I missed seeing Hunter the last time he came home.

When Ankiza hesitates, Sheena asks, "Did you break up with him?"

"Only a fool would break up with that sweet thing!" Rina states.

Ankiza gives her a complacent smile. "Hunter and I have decided to cool our relationship for a while. This long distance thing is hard and besides, I've decided to go to UCLA next year."

As if she's read my mind, Maya comments, "Ty and I won't let anything separate us, not even miles. One day we're gonna get married." Maya has such a sweet look on her face that I don't dare contradict her to tell her I'm too young to get married.

"I can hardly wait until graduation," Sheena remarks. "Then I can get me a job, move out. I can't stand being around my mom no more."

When Ankiza warns that it's almost time for the first bell, Rina rolls her window down, calling out to Rudy and Juanita who are sitting on a bench near the tiny play area. They hurry back to the car, and as we drive away, Rina accuses Rudy of farting, so they go at it again as if they were in a championship boxing match.

Of all my afternoon classes, science is my least favorite subject, but today it turns out fairly interesting. Mrs. Hopper discusses the North and South Poles, pointing out that in countries like Finland people live in darkness for six months at a time. That's crazy, I think to myself, trying to fall asleep at night when it's still light outside.

After school, I get a ride to the Teen Resource Center. When I get there, it's empty except for Jimmy and Lalo, who are playing pool while they wait for Ray's van to appear. Lalo invites me to join them, but instead I sit on the couch to read an *NBA Hoops* magazine until Ray finally arrives. Marcos is right behind him, along with Kiko, Edgar, and Kareem, who are carrying boxes of snacks.

Once we've passed around the refreshments, I help Marcos with his book report, but Jimmy right away complains that he also needs help with math. As soon as I get Marcos going on his outline, I move over to help Jimmy. Watching Jimmy struggle with simple division, I can tell he made it through elementary school without learning the basics. It's clear nobody ever took the time to help him learn.

An hour later, Ray orders everyone into the Círculo. He begins by asking how our day went, and Edgar vividly describes a fight at his school between two gangbangers.

"Man, I wanted to jump in and help Chente, but then the teacher showed up to break it up."

When Ray reminds Edgar that choices lead to consequences, I reflect on my own choices and how I got suspended from Roosevelt for the incident with Jonathan. When Marcos interrupts to say that he got a B on a math test, the door slams, and Willie enters the room. Ray begins to scold Willie for arriving late, but before he can continue, Willie's eyes fill with rage. He cries out, "You don't have to treat me like a baby!"

"Chill, *ése,*" Kiko repeats as Willie reaches down and grabs him by the shirtfront, ordering him to keep his mouth shut.

Ray is instantly on his feet, separating Willie from Kiko, whose face has turned pale. "Willie, you're outta here," Ray commands. "You know we have rules about being respectful."

We watch in astonishment as Willie lowers his head and begins to sob. Ray reaches out to embrace him, gently guiding the distraught Willie back to his office. After a few moments, Ray reappears to let us know that he's taking Willie home. "Can you stay in charge, Tyrone?" he asks, and I nod as he returns to his office for Willie.

As we watch them walk out to Ray's van, Marcos says, "I wonder what happened."

"I thought only sissies cried," Jimmy remarks.

"Shut up, dog," Lalo orders him.

Half an hour later when Ray returns, Kareem wants to know what happened. "It's Willie's dad," Ray explains. "He was killed last night. It was a freak car accident. Mr. Rivera was on his way home from work, and a semitruck crossed the yellow line, running into his car."

There is a huge knot in my stomach as I think back to my last conversation with Willie. He talked about how his dad was always there for him, even after he found out Willie was all strung out on drugs.

Later, when Ray drives me home, he asks how I'm getting along with my dad. When I tell him that we're still not speaking, Ray gives me a long hard stare, saying, "Willic never got to say good-bye to his dad. Think about it. The same thing could happen to your dad."

Fifteen

I'm halfway through a chapter on global warming when there's a tap on the door, and Dad's face appears in the cracked door. "Can we talk?"

I mumble a gruff "no," but Dad doesn't go away. He enters the room and sits on the edge of Jerome's bed.

"What do you want?" I ask harshly, wishing I'd never witnessed Willie's heart-wrenching sobs.

"We got to talk."

"We have nothing to talk about."

Dad winces, lowering his eyes for a moment before he continues. "You know I'm going to AA now. I got a sponsor, and one of the things he told me I need to do is to make amends to everyone I've hurt."

"You really think that's gonna help?" I ask bitterly, aware of the pain I'm inflicting with each word I speak.

"I already apologized to your momma. Now I'm here to ask you if you'll forgive me for hurting you the way I did."

There are tears in Dad's weary eyes as he stares at me. I want to forgive him. Instead I lash out, "Why'd you have to go and leave us like that?"

The narrow lines on Dad's forehead seem to deepen as he explains, "I had to go dry out. I went to a recovery home. I had a sickness that was eating me inside. It made me bitter and angry, and I drank instead of facing my real problems." Dad's voice breaks, so he is silent for a moment until he regains control of his emotions. "I have a disease called alcoholism. But now I'm trying to get myself straight. I got this new job at Discount Foods. The manager, Mr. Buffa, is a good man, not like those people at Ken's Market."

"I don't think you can change, Dad."

"Yes, I can, but I have to keep going to AA for my whole life. The program's gonna help me be a good father and to learn how to communicate better with you and your momma."

Staring into Dad's stricken eyes, I think back to the night he left, how he had shouted angrily at Momma that he was tired of being passed over for promotions that were given to white men hired after he was. Then I remembered Momma's story about how hard Dad's life had been growing up Black and poor in South Central with no father to help him out.

"It hurt his manhood and pride," Momma had said, trying to get me to understand, only I hadn't . . . until now.

"So what do you say, son? Can you forgive me?" Dad repeats, his eyes glistening with hope.

"I'll think about it," I mumble, focusing my eyes back on the chapter I'm reading before Dad can notice the tears welling up in my eyes.

Slowly rising to his feet, Dad whispers in a hoarse voice, "Thanks. Hopefully in time you'll see that I ain't ever gonna let the sickness take control of me again."

After Dad leaves the room, I lean back against the headboard, close my eyes, and wonder if I've done the right thing. Maybe, just maybe, I think to myself, Dad isn't a loser like I imagined.

At dinnertime, there is a lightness in my heart that I haven't felt in the longest time. Even Momma seems to notice the difference, saying that she cooked meatloaf tonight since it's my favorite.

When Jerome insists that it's his favorite too, Dad affectionately agrees with him, saying, "No one makes a finer meatloaf than your momma."

Momma smiles happily, but Zakiya frowns. "I'm on a diet that only lets me eat vegetables."

"Don't get too skinny," Momma warns.

Zakiya scoffs back, "Oh, Momma, I just wanna look good."

"For that you'll need plastic surgery!" I sarcastically remark, and Zakiya quickly tosses a pea across the table at me. As Jerome picks up a pea from his plate, Momma flashes him a warning look, so he carefully pops it into his mouth.

While we eat, Dad tells us about his new job at Discount Foods. "Mr. Buffa is starting me out at the bottom of the scale as a meat clerk, but the wages are a lot higher than what I was getting at Ken's. And Mr. Buffa's sure that with my experience, I'll get a promotion in less than a year." His face softening, Dad turns to look at Momma. "You know, Martha, maybe then you can start working part-time."

"We'll see, Jerry. My job at the hospital is good. But maybe Tyrone won't have to work no more."

Shaking my head, I tell Momma that I enjoy working and having my own spending money, adding, "I'd like to start pitching in for the snacks at the Teen Center."

Zakiya grimaces. "Why don't you help your poor sister out? I need a new pair of shoes."

"Didn't you buy a new pair of shoes last month?" Momma asks.

"Oh, those, they're not in style any more. Maybe I'm the one who should get a job."

"Yeah, with the phone company since you live on the phone!" I exclaim.

Zakiya sneers at me as Jerome joins in, asking Dad if he's old enough to get a job. Momma exchanges a smile with Dad, who explains to Jerome that he needs to wait until he's older.

Later, when Maya calls on the phone, I tell her how Dad showed up in my room to apologize, describing the entire conversation we had.

"You're really lucky, Ty," Maya sighs. "Your dad's trying to make it up to you. Some parents aren't that up-front. Like my dad, he always tells me what I want to hear instead of the truth."

"Yeah, I guess, but how do I know he's not just saying all of that so we can all feel sorry for him?"

"Don't be *tonto*, Ty!" Maya exclaims. "Do you really think he'd be going to AA meetings if he weren't serious?"

After we hang up, I go back to my room to think about what Maya said. Maybe she's right about Dad trying to be straight with me. I guess I have to give him credit for that.

Zakiya suddenly opens the door, and as I growl at her for not knocking first, she says, "Ty, I'm glad you forgave Dad."

"And who said I forgave him?"

"Whatever," Zakiya says, walking away as Momma comes up to the open door.

"Thank you, son," Momma says.

"For what?" I ask.

"For giving your dad another chance."

Noticing the warmth that has returned to Momma's eyes, I shrug my shoulders, saying, "I just hope he doesn't disappoint us again."

"Don't worry. He won't," Momma gently replies, whispering good night as she closes the door behind her.

Sixteen

Dr. Martínez

When I entered the reception area, I was surprised to find Maya standing next to Tyrone. She was wearing a white tennis skirt with a matching polo shirt with the RHS logo on it.

"Hi, Dr. Martínez," Maya said, releasing Tyrone's hand as we embraced.

"You're looking very sporty today," I commented, watching Maya's face break into a big smile. "How are you, Maya?"

"Terrific! I gave Tyrone a ride, and I wanted to say hi before I hurry back for practice. We're in the playoffs."

"Congratulations. By the way, I had the nicest conversation with your mom the other night."

Wrinkling up her pudgy nose, Maya said, "Oh. She had to cancel her classes today. She has a real bad cold. I better get going. See you later." Before she rushed out the door, Maya paused to give an embarrassed Tyrone a kiss on the cheek.

"Is Miss Maya always in that much of a hurry?" I asked Tyrone as we walked into my office.

"Yeah, sort of," Tyrone answered, picking out a comfortable spot on the couch.

"Then she's just like her mom," I said, watching Tyrone rest his hands comfortably at his side.

"I wanted to talk with you about a new mentoring program for underrepresented youth that was recently implemented at Laguna University. When I mentioned to Maya's mother that you were interested in social work, she offered to talk to one of her colleagues about your participation in the mentoring program."

"That's cool. Thanks, Dr. Martínez."

"Have you talked with your counselor, Mr. Grinde, about switching to social work?"

"Not yet, but I'm going to real soon."

"Good, because the time to apply is right now. How are things going at school?"

Tyrone sighed. "All right, I guess. Better in a way."

"What do you mean?"

"I'm almost caught up in my classes. And there's been a couple of times I wanted to take my frustrations out on Jonathan, but I didn't. I don't want to risk getting suspended again."

"I'm very pleased to hear that, Tyrone."

There was a slight pause in our conversation as Tyrone began to nervously tap his long slender fingers on the side of the couch. "My dad's home," he finally said. "He has this new job he's all excited about."

"And what about you, Tyrone, are you excited for him?"

Tyrone grew pensive. "I don't know what to think, Dr. Martínez. The other night Dad apologized. There were even tears in his eyes. Then he talked about being an alcoholic."

"How did that make you feel?" I gently pried.

Shuffling his feet in front of him, Tyrone thought about my question. After a few moments, he raised his head and stared at me intensely. "I'm not sure. I'm still angry at Dad for leaving us, but maybe he's changing. He told me he went to some place to dry out and that he's real involved with that AA stuff. He even invited me to a meeting."

"That's nice. It sounds like your dad is making some positive life changes."

"Yeah, but I don't know if I can trust him yet," Tyrone said, his anguished eyes on me again. "Momma seems to think she can trust him, so do Jerome and Zakiya, but I'm not sure yet."

"Be patient. It takes time to heal and to trust again." I thought of my own father, the endless years of trusting and hoping, only to be deceived. I prayed it wouldn't be like that for Tyrone.

Tyrone's voice called me back to his side. "Do you really think he'll change?"

"Yes, I do," I repeated despite my own nagging fears and the fact that I had fled from my father's side, refusing to give him another chance.

All of a sudden, Tyrone leaned forward, his voice thick with emotion. "Willie's dad died."

"Who's Willie?" I asked, noticing the sad expression on his face.

"He goes to the Teen Center. He's trying to get his G.E.D." Pausing for a moment, Tyrone went on to describe Willie's behavior at the Teen Center the day after the tragic accident that had killed his dad. Then, his voice barely audible, Tyrone muttered, "Willie always said his dad stuck by him, even when he was on drugs."

"I'm very sorry. Willie must be very hurt, losing his father that way."

Tyrone closed his eyes momentarily, and when he opened them, he whispered, "Maybe it's okay that Dad came back. Like Ray said, everyone deserves another chance."

"I'm glad you feel that way," I said, reaching out to pat him on the arm. Tyrone nodded, and as he rose to his feet, I complimented him on his newfound maturity.

As I prepared to leave my office, stuffing some paperwork into my briefcase, I reflected on all the young people I'd helped to empower over the years. On days like today, I felt truly confident and successful, knowing I'd made the right choice in becoming a psychologist.

Seventeen

Dr. Martínez

Turning onto Adriano St., where Frank and I had lived for almost ten years, I spotted Bryan's car parked in front of our modest three-bedroom house. Wondering why Frank hadn't called to say his older brother was in town, I pulled into the driveway and hurried out of the car, eager to see my brother-in-law.

Bryan was at my side the minute I opened the front door. "Dr. Martínez, you're looking fabulous!" he exclaimed, embracing me warmly.

"Watch out, Bryan! Sandy's a married woman," Frank teased as Diego, Bryan's partner of several years, came up to join in the family reunion.

Once we were finished with all the kissing and hugging, we went into the living room, and I quizzed them about their unexpected visit.

With a boyish grin, Bryan replied, "We're headed to an AIDS convention in LA, so I thought I'd check on my *panzón* baby brother."

Frank was on his feet in a matter of seconds, pushing out his small stomach to make it look even bigger.

"*Ay*, Frank, *eres tremendo*," Diego exclaimed in his perfect Spanish accent.

Watching Diego's handsome Mexican face, I couldn't help but think that he and Bryan were such a striking couple. With his gypsy black hair and dark-brown eyes, Diego reminded me of a young Anthony Quinn while Bryan, who was fair-skinned with sandy hair and bright blue eyes, typified the Dutch ancestry in Frank's family.

"Sandy," Bryan remarked, "Frank said you already went back to work."

Our eyes meeting, I replied, "Yes, the world would be such a mess without us shrinks."

"We've been worried about you and Frank," Diego admitted. "We know how rough things can get."

"Thanks, Diego, but we're doing much better now."

As I observed Bryan lovingly squeeze Diego's hand, I knew that they were thinking about all the tumultuous changes their relationship had survived. First, the rejection by Frank's parents, upon finding out that Bryan and Diego were a couple. Then, having to confront Bryan's illness after discovering he was HIV positive.

We were suddenly interrupted by the doorbell, and Frank rose swiftly to his feet, returning moments later with the Chinese food he had ordered.

"Chow time!" he yelled, ordering everyone into the kitchen where Bryan proceeded to open the bottle of red wine they had bought for us on their recent trip to the Napa vineyards.

While we ate, Bryan talked about the AIDS conference in Los Angeles and the newest research that would be presented there.

"Bryan, how have you been feeling lately?" Frank asked.

Diego answered for him, "He's a pain most of the time, if that's what you mean."

Smiling, Bryan said, "I'm feeling stronger again, but it's hard taking all those pills on a daily basis."

"Can you believe I'm his nurse?" Diego joked. "I put his pills out every morning and make sure he doesn't forget to take them."

"I'm very happy you have Diego," I told Bryan. They exchanged another tender look. Bryan was indeed lucky because I knew Diego loved Bryan as much as Frank loved me. Bryan and Diego were going on their sixth year together. It was obvious that nothing was going to come between them, not even HIV.

"Anyone for more chow mein, or shall I polish it off?" Frank asked, dangling his chopsticks in the air, ready to attack.

"Go ahead, *panzoncito*. Finish it off," I laughed as Frank quickly emptied out the container.

After dinner, while Diego helped Frank load the dishwasher, Bryan and I went for a short walk around the block. Our arms hooked together, we breathed in the sweet smells of jasmine as we walked in silence under the watchful eye of Orion the Hunter.

Bryan was the first to speak, "Frank told me you've been going to a grief support group."

"Yes," I sighed. "It's been our saving grace. I was beginning to think we were headed for a divorce after losing the baby, but now things are much better."

"I'm glad," Bryan said, adding, "You know, Sandy, Diego and I have been attending an HIV support group, and without that, I don't know how we would've managed. It's been a relief knowing that there are other couples like us who are going through the same painful ordeal."

"I know exactly what you mean. I wanted to die when I lost the baby, but after seeing all those other women and listening to their stories, I knew I could begin to heal, that I wasn't alone."

Bryan squeezed my arm, his clear blue eyes twinkling. "I'm glad you're well again. Now, if we could only do something about that crazy brother of mine!"

Our laughter resonanted through the star-studded night, and as we circled the block, heading back to the house, I knew in my heart that I had found a new brother in Bryan.

The next morning, by the time Frank and I got out of bed, Bryan and Diego were gone, leaving behind a note that made us both smile: *Good morning, lovebirds. Diego and I didn't want to wake you. Will call when we get back to the city. Sandy, put that* panzón *on a diet, will you?*

After Frank left, I sat down with my second cup of coffee to read the morning newspaper. I was scanning an article on the war in the Middle East when my mother called from Delano. Pursing my lips, I greeted her calmly as she asked about Frank. I told her how happy he'd been with Bryan's visit, avoiding Diego's name since I knew Mom was strongly opposed to gay relationships.

"*Es un pecado*," a sin, she'd repeated any time the subject of gays or lesbians arose in our conversation.

I was about to ask how Dad was feeling when Mom said, "*Hija*, I wanted to let you know your dad's agreed to go to an AA meeting next week."

"He has?" I asked, completely astounded by Mom's sudden news.

"Yes, *hija*. I can't believe it myself. This time I think your dad really wants to quit drinking."

I could feel the tears forming in my eyes as I whispered, "Mom, I can't believe it. I'm overjoyed to hear this."

"Yes, *hija*, me too. I've been praying and praying to San Judas. He finally answered my prayers."

"*Qué bueno, Mamá*," I replied, smiling to myself at Mom's unbending faith in her Catholic saints. She had a saint for every occasion and every illness. Who was I to challenge her beliefs?

"*Hija*," Mom continued, "I know sometimes we don't see eye to eye. But I want you to know that your dad and I love you more than anything."

"Thanks, Mom," I whispered into the receiver, wishing Andy were still here to share the good news.

Eighteen

Tyrone

On Wednesday, I've just left Inboxes, and I'm crossing through the parking lot when a car pulls up alongside of me, forcing me to stop on my tracks. Leaning his head out the window, Max says, "Hey, dude, how's the pimping at Inboxes?"

Chad, who's seated on the passenger's side, laughs, a seedy grin spreading across his pock-marked face as I answer, "It's cool."

Max asks, "Why haven't you returned any of my calls?"

"I've been busy with work and school."

"Don't sweat it, dude," he says, "You can make it up to me right now. Chad and I are going to this kegger at some chick's house. Hop in, dude."

"I can't. Momma's expecting me for dinner."

Chad sneers, "Don't be a faggot, dude." Then Chad cackles, and I want to grab him by his long skinny neck. Before I can react to Chad's stupid remark, Max pleads, "Come on, dude. Don't chicken out. It's gonna be a wild one."

Now Chad begins to make clucking sounds like a chicken, so I make a hasty decision since there's no way in hell

I'm gonna let anyone think I'm chicken. Not even some dumb-ass college guy.

"All right, I'll go," I answer gruffly, climbing into the backseat as Chad gives me an approving nod.

The party is near Laguna University in a large two-story home that appears to be a student rental. A keg of beer has been set up on the deck in the backyard, and clusters of students are drinking beer to the sounds of hip-hop music. The husky, bearded guy standing next to the keg hands each of us a glass of beer.

"Drink up," Chad orders, guzzling his beer as Max moves toward the fence, where a couple of girls are standing. Belching loudly, Chad takes off to join one of his moronic friends on the other side of the deck. As I take another drink of my beer, I begin to wonder why I ever let myself get talked into coming to this place. The beer tastes stale, and I'm in a house filled with strangers who are all trashed.

When two girls approach me, Chad is quickly at my side, making a few more obscene comments. Their eyes glazed, the two girls giggle as if Chad's sexist remarks are entertaining. Disgusted, I down the rest of my beer and make a quick exit as Chad continues sucking it up to the two Barbies.

Back outside, I walk up the nearest street, and I continue until I find a bus stop. Only then do I sigh with relief, knowing I've made the right decision in leaving the party. Drinking is definitely not my game.

Momma calls out from the living room when she hears me open the front door. She is on the couch watching the evening news with Dad. "Son, I saved you some dinner. It's on the stove."

"Good 'cause I'm starved," I answer, avoiding Dad's stare as I go into the kitchen to serve myself some of Momma's leftover steak and potatoes.

I'm opening a can of soda when Dad enters the room. "Have you been drinking?" he asks, pulling up a chair across from me.

"I had a few. So what?" I mutter and take a long drink from my Coke.

Dad sighs, his head dropping slightly. "That's all it takes."

"Yeah, I guess you oughta know," I answer stiffly.

After several moments of silence, Dad lifts his head to say, "You're right. I had this sickness all the time, but I didn't want to admit it. And that's what it is: a sickness. It takes a hold of a man and destroys him."

I can feel the hurt wrenching in Dad's heart as he goes on to explain. "Drugs and alcohol have cursed the Black community for generations. Did you know two of your uncles died from it?"

I shake my head as Dad continues, "My brother Dan choked to death on a bottle of whiskey at the age of thirty-nine, and my oldest brother, Vincent, died of a drug over-dose. Destroying ourselves, that's how we Black men have coped. That's what we done all these years."

Watching Dad's eyes fill with tears, I am suddenly ashamed of my behavior, of the way I've tried to push Dad away as if he were no good.

"I couldn't let no one call me a chicken," I hesitate, carefully describing the entire story about Max and the party. "But, once I got to the party, I realized I didn't even wanna be there. I don't even like how beer tastes."

Dad reaches out for my hand, whispering, "Praise God."

"And I know I gotta stay focused on my plans. I'm going to college, and I won't let anything mess that up."

"I'm glad to hear that, son," Dad whispers. "I'm glad you don't want to be a drunk like me and all your uncles."

Now I am the one who comes to Dad's defense. "No way you're a drunk, Dad. I'm proud to be your son."

There is a warmth in Dad's eyes as he came around the table to embrace me.

Zakiya walks into the kitchen, and her mouth drops when she sees us. "It's Maya," she finally says. "She's called about a hundred times asking where you went."

"You better hurry," Dad says, winking at me. "It's not good to keep a lady waiting."

In the hallway, I anxiously pick up the receiver, wondering what I am going to say.

"Hey, babe," I cheerfully greet Maya, who doesn't waste a second before she begins her cross-examination. When I tell her everything I told Dad, the first thing Maya wants to know is if Mickey was at the party. Amused at Maya's jealousy, I tell her no, reminding Maya that she's the only girl for me.

"Good," Maya agrees, "'cause I'll let that ho have it if she ever tries to get close to you."

Laughing into the phone, I advise Maya to take some boxing lessons. "Or how about karate?" I tease. "Maybe Rudy can teach you."

Maya cries out, "That *mosco*! *¡Olvídalo!* I'd be better off asking Mrs. Plumb!"

After I hang up with Maya, Momma calls me into the living room. "Son, they're having a barbecue after church this Sunday. Your dad and I were wondering if you'd come with us. Zakiya's coming too." I can tell by the lightness in her voice that Dad has told her about our conversation.

"Sure, Momma. Maybe Maya will come along."

When Jerome suddenly gives a loud cheer from the top of the stairway, Momma cries, "I thought I told you to get your little butt to bed!"

Dad and I exchange a smile as Momma hurries after Jerome.

Nineteen

On Thursday, Mr. Grinde calls me into his office during fifth period. He begins by complimenting me about catching up on my missed assignments. Then Mr. Grinde asks if I'm ready to fill out my application for admission into the School of Engineering at Laguna University. When I tell him I've changed my mind, Mr. Grinde frowns.

I can imagine what is going through his mind, so I hastily speak up. "Don't get me wrong, Mr. Grinde. I'm still planning on going to the university, only I'd like to get a degree in social work instead of engineering."

"You had me worried there for a minute," Mr. Grinde says, wrinkling his brow. "Are you certain about switching programs?"

Nodding, I explain that my work at the Teen Resource Center has made me realize that I'd like to help others. "I'd like to be like Ray and make a difference in someone's life."

Satisfied, Mr. Grinde reaches for his Laguna University catalog, and we look at the general education requirements for the bachelor's degree. As we go on to review the first year coursework for a degree in social work, I mention that Maya's mother is going to get me in the new mentoring program at the university. Another smile appears on Mr. Grinde's face, and as I get up to leave, he reminds me, "Fill out the admissions application before the end of the month."

Maya has a playoff match after school, so I get a ride to the Teen Resource Center with Tommy, who is on his way to the Rialto Theater to interview for a part-time job. When I walk through the door, I glance around for Marcos, but he still hasn't arrived. Ray waves at me from the corner of the room near the bookshelves, where he's talking with Lalo and Kiko.

As I join Kareem and Edgar on the couch, Jimmy looks up at me, helplessly, "Hey, *ese*, I'm trying to figure out this math problem, but it's way too hard."

"That's 'cause you're stupid," Edgar says jokingly, glancing up from his journal, which he guards like a prized trophy. Edgar likes to write poems. Sometimes he shares them with us in the Círculos, but they're full of cuss words. Still, Edgar has a way of expressing all the pain he feels in his writing. If only I could be a poet like Edgar, but I guess everyone's different.

I help Jimmy with his math until Ray calls for everyone to gather around the couch for the Círculo.

Once we're all quiet, Ray holds up a small brown book, saying, "Today, I'm going to read a chapter from *The Tiny Warrior*. It's a book by D.J. Eagle Bear Vanas. He's a Native American writer who's written this powerful book about becoming a warrior."

"Oh, man, not another book," Kiko grimaces. "I'm sick of books."

"Get *trucha*, Mr. G. Our teachers are always making us read boring books at school," Jimmy complains.

"Shut up, *pendejo*! Give Mr. Gutiérrez a chance," Edgar says, and Kareem nods in agreement.

Ray eagerly states, "You'll like this book. It's a story about Justin and how his grandfather helps him. I'm going to begin by reading the prologue."

Lalo asks, "What does 'prologue' mean?"

Edgar pokes him in the arm, saying, "Man, another *pendejo*: it's like an introduction."

Smiling, Ray begins to read, and we're introduced to Justin, a twenty-seven-year-old college dropout, who lives in Sunlight with his grandfather. One day the grandfather notices something is wrong with Justin, so he asks him about it.

Justin answers, "Everything seems so difficult, so confusing. I'm not sure why or how it all happened, but I'm lost Grandpa. I feel empty inside."

As Ray pauses, Kareem confesses that he knows exactly how Justin feels. I can't help but agree with Kareem since I've been feeling that way myself lately. Fortunately, things are beginning to turn around for me.

Ray continues in Chapter One. Grandpa tells Justin the story of Cricket, an eight-year-old Indian boy who dreams of being a warrior, but feels it's impossible because he's too small. At the end of the chapter, Justin complains that he's too old for this kind of story, but Grandpa encourages him to keep on listening.

Closing *The Tiny Warrior*, Ray hands each of us a copy of the Points of Wisdom or sayings that D.J. Vanas has included at the end of each chapter.

After he reads each one out loud, Ray asks for our comments.

Kiko is the first one to respond. "I like the first one. It makes me think of all these *vatos* at school who are always trying to pressure me to get high, but I know it's all about me, about what I can do."

"I like the one that talks about searching for answers you already possess," Edgar says. "That's a cool one. When I became a peer leader, I thought I couldn't do it, get up there and give talks in front of groups, but I did. Like it says here, it was all inside of me."

Now Ray turns to look at me. "And you, Tyrone? Which one speaks to you?"

Hesitating, I think about all the anger I felt when Dad left. "I like this one," I reply, reading out loud: "*However long or far, you cannot outrun your life's problems when those problems are within.* It's true. You have to go inside to find the solution."

"Yeah, I can relate to that one too," Lalo heartily agrees.

When Kareem pleads with Ray to read the next chapter, Edgar says, "Yeah, Mr. Gutiérrez, we wanna hear more about Cricket."

In Chapter Two, Cricket goes fishing with his uncle. When Cricket says he's afraid of never becoming a warrior, his uncle gives him a lesson based on the river water that flows in all directions. Then Justin thinks of the meaning of the flowing river and his own life. He confesses to his grandfather that he always wanted to be an engineer.

"That *vato* is *trucha*," Jimmy says as the chapter comes to an end. Closing the book, Ray promises to bring copies of the Points of Wisdom for tomorrow's Círculo.

Kareem says, "I want to be a warrior like Cricket."

Jimmy grins cockily, saying, "I'm already a warrior, *ése*. Check this out." Then Jimmy lifts up his sleeve to show off a picture of an Aztec god that is tatooed on his left arm.

Shaking his head at Jimmy, Ray tells us to gather our belongings so that he can take us home.

After we're alone in the van, I ask Ray about Marcos, and he explains that Marcos and his family had to move away because his mom found a better job near her sister in the Bay Area.

"That's cool," I answer, pleased that life will improve for Marcos and his family. Still, I can't help but feel disappointed that I won't see the little guy anymore.

"How are you and your dad getting along?" Ray carefully asks.

"Better. Last night we talked a lot."

"That's what it's all about," Ray says as we arrive at the dull brown apartment building. When I reach for the door handle, Ray asks me to wait while he takes his briefcase from the backseat and pulls out *The Tiny Warrior*.

Handing it to me, Ray says, "Here, this is for you, Tyrone. You're already on the warrior path."

Twenty

Dr. Martínez

"Did you enjoy the Lakers win last night?" I asked Tyrone as he sat across from me on the couch.

Tyrone nodded. "Yeah, it was awesome."

"Frank was going crazy with the triple overtime. I almost had to give him a sedative to calm him down. By the way, do you know if Ray Gutiérrez is a Lakers fan?"

"Nah, he's a big time Dodgers fan."

"Too bad, but to quote my husband, Frank, anyone who lives in California sooner or later becomes a Lakers fan."

Tyrone's smile faded, and the light in his eyes grew dim. "Marcos left."

"I'm sorry to hear that. I know how much you looked forward to seeing him at the center."

"Yeah, but it was the best thing for Marcos," Tyrone admitted. "Ray said his mom got a better job."

"Then I am very happy for Marcos," I said, watching Tyrone extract a small brown book from his jacket.

Handing it to me, Tyrone remarked, "Dr. Martínez, I wanted to show you this book. Ray gave it to me."

"*The Tiny Warrior*," I read aloud, noting the author's name. "Sounds intriguing."

Tyrone's voice thickened with excitement. "It's the story of a guy named Justin who dropped out of college. He's real depressed about his life, but his grandpa helps him by telling him the story of an Indian boy named Cricket. This is the best book I've ever read. I couldn't put it down until I finished it."

"It must be a powerful story," I exclaimed, reading the comments on the book jacket.

"What I like the most are the Points of Wisdom at the end of each chapter."

"Will you share one with me?" I asked, handing him *The Tiny Warrior.*

Tyrone opened the book and began to read. "*Choose your pack wisely. Your spirit is like a sponge, soaking up who and what surrounds you.*" His eyes shining like beacons, Tyrone said, "This saying reminded me of the things I was doing when I dropped out of Roosevelt. I was hanging out with Max, getting loaded, getting more depressed. Then there's the one about the spirit dogs."

"Read that one," I suggested, delighted with Tyrone's sudden enthusiasm about reading.

Turning a few more pages, Tyrone continued to read. "*The positive and negative 'spirit dogs' fight for your attitude every day. The one you feed determines the winner.*" Pausing to catch his breath, Tyrone said, "I really liked this one. It made me think about how angry I've been acting toward my dad."

"It sounds like *The Tiny Warrior* has helped you sort out your feelings."

"Yeah, it really has. It has blank pages for each chapter, so you can write your feelings down. I haven't done that yet, but I know I want to be like Justin: get a college degree and give back to the community. After reading *The Tiny Warrior*, I'm more determined than ever to be like Ray, so I can help others."

I reached out to pat Tyrone's hand, complimenting him on his self-determination and desire for social change. Capitalizing on Tyrone's positive attitude, I ask, "How are you and your dad getting along?"

After a lengthy sigh, Tyrone described the party with Max and the tense conversation that followed with his father. "But everything turned out fine. At first, I thought Dad was dissing me, but I found out he was just worried about me drinking and that I'd end up like one of my uncles. I made it crystal clear that I'm going to make something out of my life and go to college. That made him real happy. But you know what? Sometimes I'm still angry at Dad. I still have my doubts about trusting him."

"Just be patient, Tyrone. Give it some time. You've already taken an important step by listening to your dad and talking with him straight from the heart."

We spent the remainder of the session discussing Tyrone's meeting with Mr. Grinde about his college goals. Before Tyrone left, I copied D.J. Vanas' web site address with the intention of ordering myself a copy of *The Tiny Warrior*.

While I waited for my next client to arrive, I dialed my parents' number in Delano. Surprised to hear Dad's voice at the other end of the line, I asked for Mom, but he explained that she was at her *comadre* María's house.

As I was about to ask how he was feeling, Dad said, "*Hija*, I'm glad you called."

"Dad, I'm sorry I didn't go back to the hospital, but . . ."

"It's all right, *hija*," Dad interrupted in a hoarse voice. "You don't have to explain. I just want you to know how important you are to me and how much I love you."

I had to blink back the tears as I whispered, "I love you too, Dad."

Coughing softly, Dad paused to clear his voice before he went on. "Sandra, last night I went to my first AA meeting."

"You don't know how happy that makes me, Dad. Did Mom go with you?"

"She wanted to, but I wouldn't let her. Maybe later. For now, I want to try to do it on my own. *Hija,* I never thought I'd set foot in one of those meetings, but it wasn't so bad. There was a speaker who called on me to introduce myself, and for the first time, I had to admit I was an alcoholic in front of strangers."

"Dad, I want you to know that whatever it takes for you to get sober, you have all of my support, as well as Frank's. He loves you as much as I do."

"Thanks, *hija*. That means a lot to me." There was a moment of silence. Then Dad continued. "Last night I met a lot of men just like me. Some of them even went up in front of the group and told their stories. I don't know when I'll be able to do that, but I bought an AA book that has the Twelve Steps in it. They're a set of principles to live a sober life. I already shared them with your mom."

"That's great, Dad. Maybe you can share the Twelve Steps with me the next time we visit."

"*Sí, hija*, I will. Guess I shouldn't have been so stubborn about AA all these years."

"Don't worry, Dad," I reassured him. "Today is what matters, and you've already initiated the recovery process." Dad's voice broke as we said good-bye.

Hanging up the receiver, I felt suddenly lighter, as if I had released an enormous burden I'd carried inside my heart all these years.

That evening, I happily described my day to Frank, starting with Tyrone and *The Tiny Warrior*. As Frank began to congratulate me, I interrupted him, exclaiming, "Wait a minute, *panzoncito*. I'm not finished with the good news. Dad went to his first AA meeting, and he liked it."

"He did? How did that happen? Did Mom tie him up and drag him there?"

Chuckling at the idea of Mom kidnapping Dad, I answered, "No, he went on his own."

Frank stretched out his hand to stroke my cheek tenderly. "Hon, I knew your dad would come around. He's a good man, just like Tyrone's dad."

"Why, Mr. Burton, for an accountant, you're awful perceptive!" I cried as Frank's face broke into a sheepish grin.

Drawing me into his arms, Frank wiggled his tempting pink tongue in my face, saying, "Okay, woman, time for some *lengua!*"

Glossary

Ándale, hija, no seas mal agradecida—Come on, daughter, don't be ungrateful.

Bien, hija—That's fine, daughter.

Buey—dummie.

Chicana(o)—a person of Mexican descent living in the United States who has a political consciousness related to Chicana/o issues and those of other ethnic groups.

Círculo—a rap session or gathering in a group or circle format.

Comadre(s)/compadre(s)—protector; close family friend; a relative by mutual consent that may not be of blood.

D.J. Eagle Bear Vanas—author of *The Tiny Warrior.* Vanas is a nationally acclaimed motivational speaker who owns Native Discovery, Inc. He currently resides in Colorado Springs, CO.

Eres tremendo—You're too much.

Es un pecado—It's a sin.

Ésa/ése—slang word used as a greeting that means "homegirl" or "homeboy."

Familia—family.

Flojo—lazy.

Get trucha—get real or get with the program.

Hijo/a—masculine form for son; femenine form for daughter.

Híjole—Wow! My goodness! Oh my gosh!

Huevos con chorizo—eggs with Mexican sausage.

Lengua—tongue, language.

Los Tigres del Norte—one of the most prominent award-winning Mexican groups that has popularized Norteño music in the United States.

Male Voices Project—a National Organization to empower young males.

MEChA—Movimiento Estudiantil Chicano de Aztlán; an early student organization that was formed during the Chicano Movement of the 1960s.

Mosca—a fly.

Nada—nothing.

Norteñas—regional Tex-Mex music that encompasses regional ensembles and their particular styles.

¡Olvídalo!—Forget it!

Órale—Hey! Okay! Right on! All right!

Pachanga—a big party.

Panza—belly.

Panzón—fatso; a big-bellied person.

Panzoncito—my little fatso.

Paul Laurence Dunbar—famous nineteenth-century African-American poet.

Pendejo/a—idiot; fool; a stupid person.

Pobre—poor.

Problema—problem.

Qué bueno, Mamá—That's good, mother.

San Judas—St. Jude, patron saint of the impossible.

Santo Niño de Atocha—Catholic saint who protects children and drivers.

Suegra—mother-in-law.

That mosco! ¡Olvídalo!—That dweeb! Forget about him!

That's trucha—That's great, swell.

That vato's trucha—That guy's with it/smart.

Tonto—dummie.

Vatos—dudes or guys.

Ya no puede manejar. Casi perdió la vista en un ojo—He can't drive any longer. He's practically lost his sight in one eye.

Gloria L. Velásquez created the Roosevelt High School Series "so that young adults of different ethnic backgrounds would find themselves visible instead of invisible. When I was growing up, there weren't any books with characters with whom I could relate, characters that looked or talked like Maya, Juanita, or Ankiza. The Roosevelt High School Series [RHS] is my way of promoting cultural diversity as well as providing a forum for young people to discuss serious issues that impact their lives. I often will refer to the RHS Series as my 'Rainbow Series' since I modeled it after Jesse Jackson's concept of the rainbow coalition."

Velásquez has received numerous honors for her writings and achievements, such as being featured for Hispanic Heritage Month on KTLA, Channel 5, Los Angeles, an inclusion in *Who's Who Among Hispanic Americans, Something About the Author* and *Contemporary Authors*. In 1989, Velásquez became the first Chicana to be inducted into the University of Northern Colorado's Hall of Fame. The 2003 anthology, *Latina and Latino Voices in Literature for Teenagers* and *Children*, devotes a chapter to Velásquez's life and development as a writer. Velásquez is also featured in the 2006 PBS Documentary, *La Raza de Colorado*. In 2004, Velásquez was featured in "100 History Making Ethnic Women" by Sherry Park, (Linworth Publishing). Stanford University recently honored Velásquez with "The Gloria Velásquez Papers," archiving her life as a writer and humanitarian.